CHRISTMAS
AT THE CASTLE

CHRISTMAS AT THE CASTLE

BY

MARION LENNOX

MILLS
BOON

First published in Great Britain 2013
by Mills & Boon, an imprint of Harlequin (UK) Limited,
Large Print edition 2014
Eton House, 18-24 Paradise Road,
Richmond, Surrey, TW9 1SR

© 2013 Marion Lennox

ISBN: 978 0 263 24046 7

Printed and bound in Great Britain
by CPI Antony Rowe, Chippenham, Wiltshire

For Di and for Kevin
With thanks for the dancing and friendship.

CHAPTER ONE

'PLEASE, MY LORD, we *really* want to come to Castle Craigie for Christmas. It's where we were born. We want to see it again before it's sold. There's lots of room. We won't be a nuisance. Please, My Lord.'

My Lord. It was a powerful title, one Angus wasn't accustomed to, nor likely to become accustomed to. He'd intended to be Lord of Castle Craigie for as short a time as possible and then be out of here.

But these were his half-brother and -sisters, children of his father's second disastrous marriage, and he knew the hand they'd been dealt. He'd escaped to Manhattan, and his mother had independent money. These kids had never escaped the poverty and neglect that went with association with the old Earl.

'Our mum's not well,' the boy said, eagerly now as he hadn't been met with a blank refusal. 'She can't bring us back just for a visit. But when you wrote and said it was being sold and was there anything she wants… She doesn't, but we do. Our father sent us away without warning. Mary—she's thirteen—she used to spend hours up on the hills with the badgers and all the wild things. I know it sounds dumb, but she loved them and she still cries when she thinks about them. There's nothing like that in London. She wants a chance to say goodbye. Polly's ten and she wants to make cubby huts in the cellars again, and take pictures to show her friends that she really did live in a castle. And me… My friends are at Craigenstone. I was in a band. Just to have a chance to jam with them again, and at Christmas… Mum's so ill. It's so awful here. This'd be just…just…'

The boy broke off, but then somehow forced himself to go on. 'Please, it's our history. We'll look after ourselves. Just once, this last time so we can say goodbye properly. Please, My Lord…'

Angus Stuart was a hard-headed financier from Manhattan. He hired and fired at the highest level. He ran one of Manhattan's most prestigious investment companies. Surely he was impervious to begging.

But a sixteen-year-old boy, pleading for his siblings…

So we can say goodbye properly... What circumstances had pushed them away so fast three years ago? He didn't know, but he did know his father's appalling reputation and he could guess.

But if he was to agree... Bringing a group of needy children here, with their ailing mother? Keeping the castle open for longer than he intended? Being *My Lord* for Christmas. Angus stood in the vast, draughty castle hall and thought of all the reasons why he should refuse.

But Angus had been through the castle finances now, and he'd seen the desperate letters written to the old Earl by the children's mother. The letters outlined just how sick she was; how much the children needed support. According to the books, none had been forthcoming. This family must have been through hell.

'If I can find staff to care for you,' he heard himself say.

'Mum will take care of us. Honest...'

'You just said your mum's ill. This place doesn't look like it's been cleaned since your mother left three years ago. If I can find someone to cook for us and get this place habitable, then yes, you can come. Otherwise not. But I promise I'll try.'

Angus Stuart was a man who kept his word, so

he was committed now to trying. But he didn't want to. As far as Christmas was concerned, it was for families, and Lord Angus McTavish Stuart, Eighth Earl of Craigenstone, did not do families. He'd tried once. He'd failed.

As well as that, Castle Craigie was no one's idea of a family home, and he didn't intend to make it one. But for one pleading boy… For one needy family…

Maybe once. Just for Christmas.

Cook/Housekeeper required for three weeks over the Christmas period. Immediate start. Apply in person at Castle Craigie.

The advertisement was propped in the window of the tiny general store that serviced the village of Craigenstone. It looked incongruous, typed on parchment paper with Lord Craigenstone's coat of arms imprinted above. The rest of the displayed advertisements looked scrappy in comparison. Snow could be shovelled, ironing could be taken in, but there was no coat of arms on any advertisement except this one.

Cook/Housekeeper… Maybe…

'I could do that,' Holly said thoughtfully, but her grandmother shook her head so vigorously her beanie fell off.

'At the castle? You'd be working for the Earl. No!'

'Why not? Is he an ogre?'

'Nearly. He's the Earl. Earl, ogre, it's the same thing.'

'I thought you said you didn't know the current Earl.'

'The acorn doesn't fall far from the tree,' her grandmother said darkly, retrieving her beanie from the snow and jamming it down again over her grey curls. 'His father's been a miserly tyrant for seventy years. His father was the same before him, and so was his father before him. This one's been in America for thirty-five years but I can't see how that can have improved him.'

'How old is he?'

'Thirty-six.'

'Then he's been in America since he was one?' Holly said, startled.

'His mother, Helen, was an American heiress.' Maggie was still using her darkling tone—Grandmother warning Grandchild of Dragons. 'They say that's why the Earl married her, because of her money. Money was his God. Heaven knows how he persuaded such a lovely girl to come to live in his mausoleum of a castle. But rumour has it His Lordship courted her in London—he could be devastatingly charming when he wanted to be—then married her and brought her to live in this dump. What a shock she must have had.'

Holly's grandmother glared back along the slush- and sleet-covered main street, through the down-at-heel village and beyond, across the snow-covered moors to where the great grey shape of Castle Craigie dominated the skyline.

'She stuck it out for almost two years,' she continued. 'She had gumption and they say she loved him. But love can't change what's instilled deep down. Her husband was mean and cold and finally she faced it. She disappeared just after Christmas thirty-five years ago, taking the baby with her.'

'Didn't the Earl object?'

'As far as anyone could tell, he didn't seem to notice,' Maggie told her. 'He had his heir and it probably suited him that he didn't need to do a thing to raise him. Or spend any money. He never talked about her or his son. He lived on his own for years, then finally got his housekeeper pregnant. Delia. She was always a bit of a doormat.'

'She was a local?'

'She was a Londoner,' Maggie said. 'A poor dab of a thing. He brought her here as a maid at the time of his first marriage. She was one of the few servants who stayed on after Lady Helen left. Finally, to everyone's astonishment, he married her. Rumour was it stopped him having to pay her housekeeper's wages, but she did well by the old man. She worked like a slave and presented him with three children. But he didn't seem interested in them, either—they lived in a separate section of the castle. Finally the old man's behaviour got too outrageous, even for Delia. She had shocking arthritis and the old man's demands were crippling her even more. She left for London three years ago, taking the children with her, and no family has been back since.'

'Until now,' Holly ventured.

'That's right. The old Earl died three months ago and two weeks ago the current Earl turned up.'

'So what do you know about him, other than he's an American?' Holly's feet were freezing. Actually, all of her was freezing but she and Maggie had determined to walk, and walk they would.

And if this really was a job... It had her almost forgetting about her feet. 'Tell me about him.'

'I know a bit,' Maggie said, even more darkly. 'His American family is moneyed, as in really moneyed. There was an exposé in some magazine fifteen years or more back when his fiancée was killed that told us a bit more.'

'Fifteen years ago?'

'I think it was then. Someone in the village saw it in an American magazine and spread it round. According to gossip, he's been brought up with lots of money but not much else. His mother seems to have become a bit of a recluse—they say he was sent to boarding school at six, for heaven's sake. He's now some sort of financial whizz. You see him in the papers from time to time, in the financial section. But back then... Gossip said he started moving with the wrong crowd at college. His fiancée was called Louise—I can't remember her last name but I think she was some sort of society princess. Anyway, she died in Aspen on Christmas Eve. There was a fuss; that's why we saw it, a hint of drugs and scandal. Apparently she was there with Someone Else. The headlines said: Heir to Billions Betrayed, that sort of thing. He was twenty-one, she was twenty-three, but that's almost all I know. Then he went back to making money and we haven't heard much since. I have no idea why he's here, advertising for staff. I thought the castle was for sale; that he was here finalising the estate.' Maggie was starting to sound waspish, but maybe that was because she was cold, too. 'You'd best leave it alone.'

'But it's a paying job,' Holly said wistfully. 'Imagine… A nice scuttle full of coal for Christmas… Mmmm. I could just enquire.'

'You're here for a holiday.'

'So I am,' Holly said, and sighed and then chuckled and tucked her arm into her grandmother's. 'We're a right pair. You're playing the perfect Christmas hostess and I'm playing the perfect Christmas guest. Or not. We've been idiots, but if we're not to be eating Spam for Christmas, this might be a way out.'

'You're not serious?'

'What do I have to lose?'

'You'll be worked to death. No Earl in memory has ever been anything but a skinflint.' Maggie turned back to stare at the advertisement again. 'Cook/Housekeeper indeed. Castle Craigie has twenty bedrooms.'

'Surely this man wouldn't be thinking of filling the bedrooms,' Holly said uneasily.

'He's the Earl of Craigenstone. There's no telling what he's thinking. No Earl has done anything good by this district for generations.'

'But it's a job, Gran,' Holly said gently. 'You and I both know I need a job. I *have* to get one.'

There was a loaded silence. Holly knew what her grandmother was thinking—it was what they both knew. They had the princely sum of fifty pounds between them to last until Gran's next pension day. Talk about disaster...

And finally Maggie sighed. 'Very well,' she conceded. 'We do need coal and it's a miserly Christmas I'll be giving you without it. But if you're planning on applying, Holly, love, I'm coming with you.'

'Gran!'

'Why not? You've cooked in some of the best restaurants in Australia, and I've been a fine housekeeper in my time. Together...'

'I'm not asking you to work—and it's only one position they're advertising.'

'But I might even enjoy working,' Maggie said stoutly. 'I know it's twenty years since I've kept house for a living and I've never kept a castle. But there's a time for everything, and surely even the Earl can't serve Spam for Christmas dinner, which is all I can afford to give you.' She grinned, her indomitable sense of humour surfacing. 'I can see us in the castle kitchen, gnawing on the turkey carcass on Christmas Day. It might be grim but it'll be better than Spam.'

'So you're proposing we play Cinderella and Fairy Godmother in the servants' quarters, mopping up the leftovers?'

'Anything that gets spilt is legally ours,' her grandmother said sternly. 'that's servants' rules, and at Christmas time servants can be very, very clumsy.' She took a deep breath and braced herself. 'Very well. Let's try for it, Holly, lass. This Earl can't be any worse than his father, surely. What do we have to lose?'

'Nothing,' Holly agreed and that was what she thought.

How could she lose anything when she had nothing left to lose? She and her grandmother both.

'Okay, let's go home and write a couple of résumés that'll blow him out of the water,' Holly said. 'And he needn't think he's paying us peanuts. He's not getting monkeys; he's getting the best.'

'Excellent,' Maggie agreed, and Holly thought they probably had a snowball's chance in a bush-fire of getting this job, especially as they were insisting it was two jobs. But writing the résumés might keep Maggie happy for the afternoon, and right now that was all that mattered.

Because, right now, Holly wasn't thinking past this afternoon. She was even avoiding thinking past the next hour.

If no one applied as Cook/Housekeeper over the next couple of days, Lord Angus McTavish Stuart, Eighth Earl of Craigenstone, could fly back home for Christmas.

Home was Manhattan. He had a sleek apartment overlooking Central Park and Christmas plans were set in stone. Since Louise had died he'd had a standard booking with friends for Christmas dinner at possibly the most talked about restaurant on the island. He'd make his normal quiet drive the next day to visit his mother, who'd be surrounded by her servants at her home in Martha's Vineyard. She loathed Christmas Day itself but reluctantly celebrated the day after with him. Then the whole fuss of Christmas would die down.

'If no one applies by tomorrow, I'm calling it

quits,' he told the small black scrap of canine misery by his side. He'd found the dog the first day he'd been here, cringing in the stables.

'It's a stray—let me take it to the dog shelter, My Lord,' his estate manager had said when he'd picked it up and brought it inside, but the scruffy creature had looked at him with huge brown eyes and Angus had thought it wouldn't hurt to give the dog a few days of being Dog of the Castle. Angus was playing Lord of the Castle. Reality would return all too soon.

The little dog looked up at him now and he thought that when he left the dog would have to go, too. No more pretending. Meanwhile…

'Have another dog biscuit,' Angus told him, tossing yet another log onto the blazing fire. The weather outside was appalling and the old Earl had certainly never considered central heating. 'This place is on the market so we're both on borrowed time, but we might as well be comfortable while we wait.'

The little dog opened one eye, cautiously accepted his dog biscuit, nibbled it with delicacy and then settled back down to sleep in a way that told Angus this room had once been this dog's domain. But his father had never kept dogs.

Had his father ever used this room? It seemed to Angus that his father had done nothing but lie in bed and give orders.

Who knew which orders had been obeyed? Stanley, the Estate Manager, seemed to be doing exactly what he liked. Honesty didn't seem to be his strong suit. Angus's short but astute time with the estate books had hinted that Stanley had been milking the castle finances for years.

But he couldn't sack him—not now. He was the only servant left, the only one who knew the land, who could show prospective purchasers over the estate, who could sound even vaguely knowledgeable about the place.

Angus had decided he'd do a final reckoning after the castle was sold and not before. His plan had been to get rid of the castle and all it represented and leave as fast as he could. This place had nothing to do with him. He'd been taken away before his first birthday and he'd never been back.

But first he had to get through one Christmas— or not. If he could find a cook he'd stay and do his duty by the kids. Otherwise, Manhattan beckoned. The temptation not to find a cook was huge, but he'd promised.

A knock on the great castle doors reverberated through the hall, reaching through the thick doors of the snug. The little dog lifted his head and barked, and then resettled, duty done. If this castle was to be sold, then there was serious sleeping to be got through first.

Stanley's humourless face appeared around the door. 'I'll see to it, My Lord,' he said. 'It'll be one of the villagers wanting something. They're always wanting something. His Lordship taught me early how to see them off.'

He gave what he obviously thought was a conspiratorial nod and closed the door again. His footsteps retreated across the hall towards the great door leading outside.

Angus opened the snug door and listened.

'Yes?' Stanley's voice was as dry and unwelcoming as the man himself. As apparently the old Earl had encouraged him to be.

'I'm here about the advertisement for help over Christmas.' Surprisingly, it was a woman's voice, young, cheerful and lilting, and Angus leaned on the door jamb and wondered how long it had been since he'd heard a woman's voice. Only two weeks, he conceded, but it seemed as if he'd been locked in this great grey fortress for ever.

He could see why his mother had fled. The wonder of it was that she'd stayed for two years.

'You look very young to be a cook,' Stanley was saying dourly, to whoever it was outside the door. Stanley's disapproval was instant and obvious, even at a distance. 'Do you have any qualifications?'

'I'm not a cook; I'm a chef,' the woman said. 'I'm twenty-eight and I've been working with food since I was fifteen. I've worked in some of the best restaurants in Australia so I'm overqualified for this job, but I have a few weeks to spare. If you're interested…'

'Can you make beds?' Stanley asked, even more dourly.

'No.' The woman sounded less confident now she wasn't talking of cooking. 'Or at least I can pull up a mean duvet but not much more. My grandmother, on the other hand, used to be the housekeeper at Gorse Hall, and she's interested in a job, too. She can make really excellent beds.'

'This is one job,' Stanley snapped. 'His Lordship wants someone who can cook *and* make his bed.'

'So is it just His Lordship I'm cooking for? Can't His Lordship make his own bed?'

'Don't be impertinent,' Stanley retorted. 'You're obviously not suitable.' And, with that, Angus heard the great doors starting to creak closed.

That should be the end of it, he told himself with a certain amount of relief. He'd agreed to advertise for a cook. He'd put the advertisement in the window of the general store and no one had replied until now. So be it. Once Stanley had got rid of her he could ring his half-brother and say regretfully, *Sorry, Ben, I couldn't find someone suitable and I can't put you up for Christmas without staff. I'll arrange to fly you and your family up to do a tour before the castle is sold, but that's all I can do.*

Easy. All he had to do was keep quiet now.

But… *Can't His Lordship make his own bed?* What was it about that blunt question that had him stepping out of the snug, striding over the vast flagstones of the Great Hall, intercepting Stanley and stopping the vast doors from closing.

Seeing for himself who Stanley was talking to.

The girl on the far side of the doors looked cold. That was his first impression.

His second impression was that she was cute.

Very cute.

She was five feet three or five four at most. She

wasn't plump, but she wasn't thin—just nicely curved, although she was doing a decent job of disguising those curves. She was wearing faded jeans, trainers, a thick grey sweater and a vast old army greatcoat without buttons. She wore a red beanie with a hole in it. A few strands of burnt-copper curls were sneaking through. Her lack of make-up, her clear green eyes and her wide, generous mouth which, at the moment, was making a fairly childlike grimace at Stanley, made him think she couldn't possibly be twenty-eight.

Maybe Stanley was right to reject her out of hand. What sort of person applied for a job wearing what looked like charity rejects?

'Are you backup?' she queried bitterly as he swung the door wider. Whatever else she was, this woman wasn't shy, and Stanley's flat rejection had seemingly made her angry. 'Are you here to help Lurch here tell me to get off the property fast? I've walked all the way from the village on your horrible pot-holed road. Of all the cold welcomes… You could at least look at my résumé.'

Lurch? The word caught him. Angus glanced at Stanley and thought the woman had a point—there were definite similarities between his

father's estate manager and the butler from the
Addams Family.

'It *is* only the one job,' he said, and found himself sounding apologetic.

'Chef and Housekeeper for this whole place?'
She stood back and gestured to the sweep of the
vast castle. The original keep had been built at the
start of the thirteenth century, but a mishmash of
battlements, turrets and towers had been added ad
hoc over the last eight hundred years. From where
she was standing, she couldn't possibly take it all
in—the great grey edifice was practically a crag
all by itself. 'This place'd take me a week to dust,'
she said and then stood back a bit further. 'Probably two. And I'm not all that skilled at dusting.'

'I don't want anything dusted,' Angus told her.

'I'm not serving my food on dust.'

'Forgive me.' He was starting to feel bemused.
This woman looked a waif but she was a waif with
attitude. 'And forgive our cavalier treatment of
you. But you don't look like a cook to us.'

'That's because I'm a chef,' she retorted. Her
cheeks were flushed crimson and he thought it
wasn't just the cold. Stanley's rejection was smarting.

'Can you prove it?'

'Of course.' She hauled a couple of typed sheets from the pocket of her greatcoat, handed them over and waited while he unfolded and skimmed them.

He felt his brows hike as he read. This was impressive. Really impressive. But…

'You're asking us to believe you're a chef from Australia—yet your résumé is typed on letterhead paper from the Craigenstone Library.'

'That's because Doris, the librarian, is a friend of my grandmother,' she said patiently. 'I'm here on holiday, visiting my Gran, and Gran doesn't have a printer. For some weird reason, I failed to bring copies of my résumé with me.'

'So why are you applying for a job?'

'It seems I'm not,' she said. 'Lurch here has told me you're not interested, so that's it. Meanwhile, I'm freezing. You've made me stand in six inches of snow while you've checked out my résumé and I've had enough. Merry Christmas. Gran was right all along. Bah, humbug to you both.'

And she turned and stalked off.

Or she would have stalked off if she had sensible shoes with some sort of grip, but the canvas trainers she was wearing had no grip at all. The cobbles were icy under the thin layer of freshly fallen snow. She slipped and floundered, and she started falling backward.

She flailed—and Angus caught her before she hit the ground.

One minute she was stomping off in righteous indignation. The next she was being held in arms that were unbelievably strong, gazing up into a face that was…that was…

Like every fairy tale she'd ever read. This was the Lord of Castle Craigie. She could see why the old Earl had been able to coerce women to marry him, she thought, dazed. If Gran was right, if the acorn hadn't fallen far from the tree, if this guy was like all the Earls before him…

Tall, dark and dangerous seemed an understatement. This guy was your quintessential brooding hero, over six feet tall, with lean, sculpted features, hard, chiselled bone structure, deep grey eyes, strong mouth and jet-black hair.

He was wearing a gorgeous soft tweed jacket. What was more, he was wearing a kilt! Oh, my…

But Gran had told her the current Earl was American. What was an American doing wearing a kilt?

According to Gran, he'd been an indulged but

lonely child. Apart from some scandal with a dead fiancée, he seemed only interested in making money. He'd sounded aloof, alone, like his father before him.

She'd been prepared to dislike him on sight, but sight wasn't being very helpful right now. None of his background stood out on his face. None of those things seemed important.

Oh, that kilt…

'Are…are you really the Earl?' He was cradling her as if she were a child, and for some reason it was the only thing she could think of to say. *Are you really the Earl?* How stupid was that?

'Yes,' he said and the edges of his wide mouth quirked into what was almost a smile. 'But only for a few weeks.'

'You're American.'

'Yes.'

'So why are you wearing a kilt?'

What was she doing? She should be saying, *Thank you for stopping me falling but you can put me down now.* She should say any number of things regarding the way he was holding her, but he'd scooped her up, he was holding her against his barrel-strong chest and, for a moment, for just a moment, Holly was letting herself disappear into fantasy.

She'd tell this to Maggie. *He swept me up into his arms, Gran, and oh, he was gorgeous...*

Maggie would toss a bucket of cold water over her.

Reality hit as hard as her grandmother's imaginary water, and she wriggled with intent. Reluctantly, it seemed, he set her onto her feet again, but he didn't let her go. The ground was still slippery and his hands stayed firmly on her shoulders.

'American or not, for now I'm Laird of the Castle,' he told her, smiling down at her. It was a killer smile. It made her insides…

Well, enough. She had enough to tell Maggie without letting her imagination take her further.

And Maggie would remind her sharply—as she'd told her last night, 'He's not our Laird. Most owners of estates in Scotland are referred to as Lairds or Himself, because they care for the land, and for the people they employ. Not him. We've never had a Lord who came close to being Himself. Don't you trust him an inch, lass. Not one inch.'

'We've been showing buyers over the estate,' he was saying, cutting over her thoughts. 'International buyers. For some reason, the realtor thinks it's important for me to look Scottish. My father has a room full of family tartan, kilts for all sizes, so I've been striding along beside would-be buyers, grunting, trying not to sound American, while Stanley here has been answering questions in his broadest Scottish brogue. Which is why I'm looking like the Lord of All He Surveys, off to round up my trusty men for a spot of pillaging of the surrounding villages. Pure fantasy.' He grinned. 'Right. I've told you mine, now it's your turn. Holly McIntosh, if you're a skilled chef, why are you standing on my doorstep asking for a job wearing sodden canvas trainers and a greatcoat that looks like it was worn during World War One?'

'Because I'm indulging in *my* fantasy of not freezing for Christmas,' she said, so flustered she let honesty hold sway. *Don't trust,* Gran had told her. She should have added, *Keep twenty feet away.* 'Can you let me go? I need to get home before my feet drop off from frostbite.'

'Come in,' he said, gently now, almost seductively, and she shivered.

'I need…'

'To get warm. You came to apply for a job. Let's

think about both. I have a blazing fire inside, hot tea or whisky if you prefer, cake—bought fruit cake admittedly, but at least it's cake—and Stanley will drive you back to the village when we're finished.'

'Finished what?' she demanded, maybe stupidly, but, to her astonishment, his smile broadened. The twinkle in those dark eyes seemed pure mischief. Dangerous mischief.

'When I've had my wicked way with you. Of course, being Lord of Castle Craigie, I've had my wicked way with every maiden in the village.' And then he chuckled, a lovely deep chuckle that matched his smile exactly. 'Sorry,' he said as he saw her expression. 'there's my fantasies running away with me again. That's the man in the kilt speaking, not me.'

'You're...' She could barely get her voice to work. 'You're not usually into wicked ways?'

'Nope. That's my kilt-wearing dark side. The normal me wears chinos, and I swear I'm not into pillaging at all.' He held up his hands as if to say, *Look, I'm unarmed and innocent*—which he didn't look at all. 'But I'm leaving my dark side out in the snow for now. I'll change back into Angus Stuart, Corporate Financier from Manhattan, if it reassures you. It's what I've been up to now and I'll be again soon. But please, Miss McIntosh, come in and get warm and let me re-read your résumé.'

Whoa. She took a deep breath, trying to recover from the way his arms had felt—were feeling. From the way that beguiling smile made her feel. From the sheer size and presence of the man. And the way that kilt…

Aagh. Stick to your guns, she told herself, des-perately. *Don't trust.* You're here to apply for a job—two jobs—and you're useless unless you stick to what you intended.

Useless.

The adjective swirled, bringing her back to re-ality with a sickening thud. *Useless* was the word that had been hanging over her for months. That and *stupid.*

Stick to what you need.

'It's two jobs or nothing,' she managed.

'Sorry?' Angus said, confused.

'I said, this is two jobs. I'm only interested in one, and I'm only interested if you accept us both. I won't clean. I'll cook all you like but nothing else. Gran's attending a funeral or she'd be here with me but she's applying as well. I have her résumé with me, too.'

'It's just the one job!' All this time Stanley had been standing to the side, glaring at this intrusion to his territory, but now he'd decided it was time to intercede. 'We advertised one position, My Lord. I'm sure we can find some other woman to take the role.'

'Not before Christmas, we can't,' Angus said. 'No one's applied since we've had the advertisement up.'

'It's still the one job,' Stanley said flatly.

'Right,' Holly said, reality slamming back. Oh, her feet were cold. 'That's that then. Thank you for your offer of whisky and fruit cake—and even taking your kilt off!—but we're wasting each other's time. Merry Christmas to you both and goodbye.'

And with that she hauled away from Angus's hold, turned and stomped—gingerly—away.

'If you'd really wanted a cook you should have used the newspapers,' Stanley said dourly as they watched her go.

He should have, he conceded. If he'd really wanted a cook.

He didn't want a cook. If he found a cook he'd be obliged to have his half-siblings here for Christmas. He'd be obliged to turn this castle into a home, even if it was only for three weeks.

He didn't want to.

Why?

Because, kilt or not, this place wasn't fantasy as much as tragedy. Black tragedy. His mother had pleaded with him not to come, and she'd be devastated if he extended his stay.

And he did not want a family Christmas. He didn't do Christmas. Had Louise's death and his mother's tragedy taught him nothing?

He was watching Holly stomp back across what had once been the site of a drawbridge but was now a snow-covered cobbled path and something inside him was twisting. He watched the determined set of her shoulders and he thought how she'd walked all the way from the village in canvas trainers to apply for a job he didn't want to give.

He should have said no to Ben.

He shouldn't even have come himself. He'd been stunned by his mother's reaction, her emotion as raw as if the tragedy had happened last week rather than over thirty years ago.

'Don't go near that place. Sell it fast, to the highest bidder. You don't need it. Give the money to charity—I don't care—just get rid of it, Angus.'

But he'd wanted to see.

He was the new Earl of Craigenstone. He had no intention of taking up the title, but still he wanted to see what he was letting go—as his half-brother and -sisters wanted to revisit what they were letting go. They'd lived in this place until three years ago. Their father had barricaded the place against them when their mother left, but they'd have memories and they wanted to see.

Please... The plea had been heartrending.

This wasn't about him, he thought savagely. The old Earl had had four children. Why was it just him making the decisions?

So... He'd just been offered staff. Why refuse? Personal selfishness? *Just like his father?*

He was watching Holly McIntosh march away from the castle with as much dignity as she could muster and he was thinking of his father's reputation. Mean. Selfish.

He was not like his father. Surely.

This was only for three weeks and then it'd be done. Surely his mother could cope if he ex-

plained. Surely it was time they both rid themselves of demons.

Decide now, he told himself, and he did.

'Holly...' His voice rang out over the crisp white
snow, and she heard even though she was two
hundred yards away.

She turned and glared, her hands on her hips.
This was no normal employee, he thought. If he
hired her, he'd be hiring spirit.

Christmas spirit? Holly. The thought had him
bemused.

'It can be two jobs,' he conceded, but her hands
stayed on her hips and her belligerence was obvious.

'Wages?' she called, not moving.

'What's the standard wage around here for a
cook?' he demanded of Stanley and Stanley glared
at him as if he was proposing spending Stanley's
money instead of the estate's. The figure he threw
at him sounded ridiculously low.

And...*I'm a chef.*

Holly's words had been an indignant claim to
excellence and pride had shown through.

If he employed her he'd have a chef for Christmas. And a housekeeper. Christmas. He thought
of his father's reputation and he looked at Stan-

ley's dour face and he thought that some things had to change, right now.

'I'll pay you three times basic cook's wages and I'll hire you and your grandmother as a team,' he called. And then, as Holly's expression didn't change, he added, 'I'll pay the same rate to you both.'

'My Lord!' Stanley gasped, but he was ignored. Holly's expression was changing. She was trying not to look incredulous, he realised, but she was failing. 'Each?'

'Yes.' He grinned, seeing her inner war. 'Eight-hour days and half days off on Sunday. It's three weeks of hard work, but the money will be worth it. I can't say fairer than that.'

She took a deep breath. He could see she was searching for the indignant, assertive Holly he'd seen up until now, but his offer seemed to have sucked all indignation out of her.

'Are…are meals and accommodation included?' she ventured, sounding cautious. Very cautious. As if he might bite.

'I guess. But why do you need accommodation?'

'We don't have a car,' Holly told him. 'And, in case you haven't noticed, it's snowing and your driveway is a disgrace. It took me half an hour to trudge up here and Gran's not as young as she used to be.' She tilted her chin and met his gaze head on. 'And our accommodation has to be heated.'

'Heated!' Stanley gasped, as though the word was an abomination, and Angus thought of the freezing, musty bedrooms throughout the castle, and the great draughty staircases and how much effort and expense it would take to get this place warm by Christmas. The snug had the only fireplace that didn't seem to be blocked.

But Holly was glaring a challenge and all of a sudden he was thinking of his half-brother and -sisters, who'd lived for years under these conditions, with the old man's temper as well, and he thought...maybe he could put the effort in. Maybe he could make the place less of a nightmare for them to remember. *He was not his father.*

'Done,' he said. 'With one proviso.'

'Which is?'

'That you come in now, dry out and tell me why you're wearing those stupid sodden shoes.'

'I need to get back to Gran.'

'We'll drive you back in a few minutes,' he said, goaded. 'But I'll dry you out first. I believe I just hired you. You're therefore my employee. You can sue me if you're injured on the way to and from work, so I'm looking after my investment. Come into my castle, Miss McIntosh, and we'll talk terms.'

'And have some of that fruit cake?' For heaven's sake, he thought, stunned. She sounded hungry!

'I believe that can be arranged.'

'Then your offer is gratefully accepted,' she said and trudged back towards them. She reached the front steps and Angus walked down to meet her. He held out his hand to steady her as she climbed the icy stone steps. She stared at his hand for a long moment and then she shook her head.

'I'll do this on my own terms, if you don't mind,' she said briskly. 'I need your job. I'd also quite like your fruit cake, but I don't need anything else.'

'Nothing?'

'Nothing.' She peeped a smile at him and he saw the return of a mischief that he suspected was a latent part of this woman. 'So any thought that you might be having your wicked way with the hired help, put out of your mind right now, Lord Craigenstone. Just leave that dark side you're talking about outside. I might be coming to live in your castle, but I know my rights. Also, I've just been burned. Ravishment isn't in any employment contract I intend to sign, now or ever.'

CHAPTER TWO

INSIDE, ENSCONCED IN one of the huge fireside chairs in the snug, her hands cradling a mug of hot chocolate, Holly seemed even younger than first impressions. And even more cute. Once she'd ditched the army greatcoat, he could see even more of her. Her cropped copper curls rioted as soon as she took off her beanie. They matched her cheeks which, in the warmth of the snug, grew even more flushed than they'd been when she was losing her temper out in the snow.

She concentrated on her hot chocolate and fruit cake. She ate three slices while Angus reread her résumé and then read her grandmother's.

This might work. According to the résumés, Holly could definitely cook and her Gran could definitely clean. They might even have the skills to provide him with a decent Christmas.

But her appearance didn't fit. He glanced again at her résumé. She was a cook—no, a chef—but she was looking like something the cat had dragged in. The little dog had sidled across to her when she sat down. He'd leaped up on her knee and she was fondling him while still cradling the last of the warmth from the hot chocolate.

They looked waifs and strays both.

'If you're who you say you are,' he said slowly, 'you must be one of the best paid chefs in Australia.'

'I am,' she said and then corrected herself. 'I was.'

'Can I verify this?'

She glanced at her watch. 'Yes,' she said decisively. 'I'd like you to. It's midday here. That makes it nine at night in Sydney. I have contact numbers for the head chefs for all of the last three but one of the restaurants where I've worked. On a Monday night at this time of year, most chefs will be in their kitchens. Phone them. I'll wait.'

'But I can't phone the last?' he asked, homing in on detail.

'The last place I owned myself,' she said bluntly. 'With my partner. It didn't work out.' She hesitated and then decided on honesty. 'He was my fiancé and business partner. He robbed me.'

'I'm sorry.'

'Don't be. Ring the others.'

He glanced at her and saw her face set in a mulish expression. She wanted him to ring, he thought, and with a sudden flash of insight he knew why. She was looking like a waif and she knew it. Putting herself on a professional footing would be important for her pride.

So he rang as she ate yet more fruit cake, and he received an unequivocal response from all three chefs. Three variations of a common theme.

'If you have Holly McIntosh you have a godsend. I'd hire her back in a minute. We've heard her place here has gone belly-up. Tell her the minute she gets back to Australia there's a job waiting.'

He disconnected from the last call. She was watching him gravely, and he could see she'd settled. She was on a more solid footing now.

'You want to explain the trainers?' he asked. She'd kicked off her sodden shoes and the socks beneath. She'd done it surreptitiously, kicking them under the chair and then tucking her feet up under her, but it hadn't been surreptitious enough. Her feet would be freezing, he thought. She'd been standing in sodden canvas on ice. 'Why the soaking footwear?'

'I arrived here two days ago,' she said. 'But my

baggage is still cavorting somewhere around the world. The airline says they'll find it—eventually. None of Gran's clothes fit so I'm stuck.'

'You don't think you should buy yourself some decent footwear while you wait?'

'I don't have any money,' she said flatly. 'That's why I need the job.'

'Not even enough for a pair of wellingtons?'

She took a deep breath, stared into the remains of her hot chocolate and then laid her mug down on the side table with a decided thunk. Those clear green eyes met his with an honesty he was starting to expect.

'I'm a chef,' she said. 'A good one. I and my... my ex-partner decided to set up on our own. We bought a restaurant, a great little place overlooking Sydney Harbour. We did the finances and were sure we could do it. We put everything we owned into it, or rather I did because it turned out Geoff didn't have the money he said he did. He was my fiancé. I trusted him, but I was a fool. I thought we had double the capital we had but he lied. Anyway, a month ago the creditors moved in and Geoff moved out. Fast. I don't know where he is now, but my credit cards are maxed out, I'm in debt to my ears and I'm suffering from a bad case of shattered pride. Not to mention a broken heart, although it's a bit hard to think I loved someone who turned out to be a toe-rag.'

'So you came to Scotland?' he asked incredulously. 'How does that make sense?'

'See, here's the thing,' she said slowly. 'I'm only Scottish through my Scottish dad—the rest of me's pure Australian—but I have Scottish pride and so does my very Scottish Gran. My parents died in a car crash when I was twelve. My mother's mother took me in, but she died last year. Now Maggie's the only relative I have left and when I rang her last month and sort of implied I was in trouble and due to have a dreary Christmas I didn't need to tell her exactly *how* broke I was. She guessed. So, Maggie being Maggie, she went out and bought me a plane ticket to visit.'

'She sounds great.'

'She is great,' she said warmly, and then managed a grin. 'And she's an awesome housekeeper.'

'Yet another reference,' Angus said and smiled back and thought, *That smile...*

Whoa...

'Unfortunately,' Holly went on, seemingly oblivious to the crackling electricity generated by that smile, 'what I didn't know is that Maggie's only renting her cottage. I've always thought she owned it, but no. She's not exactly known for saving, my Gran—as in the extraordinary gesture of my plane ticket. Anyway, it only took me five minutes after I'd landed to find out her landlord has put her house up for sale. She's desperately scraping enough money together to pay for a deposit to rent somewhere else, and she's as broke as I am. She thought if I flew over we could share Christmas expenses, but how do you share nothing? So that's that. We had a problem but you've solved it. You see me here in sodden trainers, but they'll dry out. You've promised us heating and we'll have a very nice Christmas because of you. Now, if you could tell me when you want me to start…'

'Do you have your airline ticket with you?' he demanded and she looked confused.

'What? Why?'

'Is it still in your purse?' he added, gesturing to her capacious handbag. 'You haven't thrown it out?'

'No, but…'

'Can I see it?'

'You want to prove that, too?' She was still confused.

'Indulge me,' he said, and she frowned and shifted the little dog, but not very far. She fumbled in her bag and found a crumpled booking sheet and airline ticket.

'Keep those toes warm while I do some more phoning,' he said, and she listened and hugged the dog some more while he phoned.

He was ringing the airline.

When she'd tried, she'd been put on hold for hours, but the Earl of Craigenstone was not put on hold. It seemed he was a member of some sort of platinum club and within seconds he was talking to…a person! Holly's jaw just about dropped to her ankles. How did you ring an airline and get a person? Oh, to be an Earl.

What was more, the person on the end of the line seemed inclined—even eager—to assist. Angus sent a few incisive questions down the line, then handed the phone over to her.

'All sorted,' he said. 'Listen.'

So Holly listened, stunned.

'We're so sorry, miss,' the man on the other end of the line said. 'This should have been explained to you. Seeing your baggage has been missing for over twenty-four hours, you can spend what you need right away and you'll be reimbursed within four working days. It also seems your grandmother has paid an extra ten pounds insurance for baggage cover so there's no loss at all—you'll get full reimbursement if the baggage isn't found, plus a small amount extra for inconvenience. I apologise that this wasn't explained to you two days ago.'

'I...thank you,' she managed and Angus took the phone from her grasp, added a few contact details and disconnected.

'So now you can buy wellingtons,' he said.

'I...' She fought for something to say and couldn't. She stared at her feet. 'Um...'

'Just how broke are you?' he asked gently and she flushed, but there seemed no point denying things now.

'Um...really, really broke,' she whispered. 'Geoff maxed out my credit cards. I owe money to everyone and Gran used her grocery money to buy my plane ticket. I...thank you but I still can't buy wellingtons because no shop will take an airline's promise that the money's coming. But I can wait four days.'

'You can't. Here's a loan to tide you over.' He hauled out his wallet, counted out a wad of notes and held them out.

'No.' What was she thinking? For some reason, her Gran's warning came slamming back and she stood up and backed to the door. 'You've given me a job. I can't take any more.'

'This isn't a gift,' he said mildly. 'When the airline pays you, you can pay me.'

'You don't know me. How can you trust me?'

'You're my employee.'

'Yes, and Geoff was my partner and look what he did,' she snapped. 'I could walk out the door and spend this on riotous living and you'd never see me again.'

'In Craigenstone?' He grinned. 'In case you hadn't noticed, there's not a lot of riotous living to be done in this place.'

He was looking at her oddly. She caught herself—she needed to make an effort to recover.

Wicked ways. Kilts and brawny arms and a wicked smile. Her imagination and the reputation of the Earl of Craigenstone were doing stupid things to her senses. Pull yourself together, she told herself and somehow she did.

'I had…I had noticed,' she said and managed to smile. She looked down at the proffered notes. Warm feet…

'This is…wonderful. I could buy myself some wellingtons and a woolly jumper and some coal.'

'You have no heating?'

'Um…no.'

'I'll run you back to the village and we'll collect some coal on the way.'

'You're kidding. You're an Earl!'

'I didn't think Australians held with the aristocracy,' he said, bemused. 'Americans certainly don't.'

'Yet you are one.'

'Only until this place is sold,' he said, humour fading. 'I intend the title to disappear with it.'

'So Gran's ogre disappears?'

'I'm an ogre?'

'That's why I'm not letting you buy coal or drive me home,' she said. 'It's very nice of you, as is lending me this money, and I appreciate it very much, but if Gran opened the door and an Earl was standing on her doorstep, loaded with coal, she'd have a palsy stroke. Whatever that is.'

'A palsy stroke?' he said dubiously.

'I hear that's what they had in the olden days,' she explained. 'When Earls knew their place and servants knew theirs. Swooning and palsy strokes were everywhere and I don't have my smelling salts with me. So no. I know my place. Gran and I will keep to the servants' quarters and cook and dust while you're all elsewhere and I'll keep to my kitchen, and you'll hand over menus of twenty courses to be cooked in two hours, and Gran will creep in at dawn and light your fires...'

'You've been reading too many romance novels if you think I want servants creeping in at dawn...'

'That's as it may be,' she said with asperity. 'But Gran has a very clear idea of what's right and wrong and we'll do this her way or not at all. So thank you but we'll buy our own coal. When would you like us to start?'

'Tomorrow?'

'Tomorrow!'

'It's two weeks until Christmas,' he said and looked ruefully round the room. 'This room and my bedroom seem the only places that are habitable. The castle's been under dust-sheets since my stepmother left. Any cooking's been done by Stanley on a portable gas ring—heaven knows if the range still works.'

'I need a stove!'

'That's why I want you tomorrow—we may

need to order one fast. Meanwhile, I need to get the place warm…'

'That'll take a year!'

'I'll do my part,' he said. 'Can you do yours, Miss McIntosh?'

'Holly,' she said, 'My Lord.'

'Angus,' he said back.'

'It's Holly and My Lord,' she said primly. 'Gran won't stand for anything else. The British Empire was built by those who knew their place and didn't step out of it.'

'So you intend to be subservient.'

'That's the one,' she said cheerfully. 'As long as you do what I tell you, I'll be as subservient as you like.'

'As long as *I* do what *you* tell me…'

'If I have a cooking range that hasn't been used for years I'll be telling you right, left and centre,' she said and rose and shoved her feet determinedly back into her soggy trainers. 'Thank you very much, My Lord. Gran and I will see you at nine tomorrow, and Christmas will begin then.' She reached out and shook his hand, then reached down and patted the little dog. 'Goodbye until then,' she said. 'Twenty courses or not, suddenly we're going to have a very yummy Christmas.'

* * *

Angus stood in the doorway and watched her go. She'd refused his offer to drive her; she'd refused his offer to send Stanley and she was trudging down the road towards the village looking like a bereft orphan thrown out into the snow.

A bereft orphan with spirit.

'You've made a mistake, My Lord,' Stanley said gloomily. He'd appeared—gloomily—behind him. 'She'll cost you a fortune.'

'Tell me, Stanley,' Angus said, in a voice any of his colleagues would have recognised and snapped to wary attention. 'How much do we have in the petty cash account?'

'I...'

'We have the rent roll from the cottages for the last month, I assume,' Angus said. 'That should cover our costs nicely. I suspect it's far too late to get central heating installed into this place by Christmas but I want every chimney swept, I want coal in every fireplace and I want oil heaters in every room. After Christmas I may need to reforest a small nation to nullify any environmental impact, but this castle *will be warm by Christmas.* Can I leave that to you, Stanley?'

His voice was silky-smooth. He was watching

Stanley's face and he knew exactly what the man was thinking.

The rent rolls for this place were colossal. They were supposed to come into a cash account at the start of the month, then roll over at the end of the month into one of his father's income-bearing accounts. What he suspected Stanley was doing and seemed to have been doing for years was siphoning the rent roll into his own account for the thirty days. Angus's father must never have noticed, but Angus thought of the interest Stanley must have earned over the years he'd been employed...

However...Stanley had put up with his father, and somehow he'd held the estate together. And he couldn't sack him now—he needed him. But then he thought of Holly in her soggy trainers and he thought of the misery caused by dishonesty everywhere.

Stanley would need to scramble to get that money back into the account, he thought, hit by a wave of sudden anger. The reputation of the miserliness of the Earl of Craigenstone stopped right now. Dishonesty stopped now, too. Up until now he'd tolerated a bit of petty theft, he'd tolerated Stanley's surliness because to change things in the short time he had here had seemed pointless. But now… Now things did need to change. Suddenly Castle Craigie was aiming for a Very Merry Christmas.

'He's nice… He's lovely and he's hired us both. At such a salary! Each!'

Holly practically bounced into the kitchen, where Maggie had been disconsolately staring at a packet of pasta and an unbranded can of tomatoes. Now she stared as if her granddaughter had lost her mind.

'What?'

Holly told her the salary and then repeated it for good measure. 'And we start tomorrow. We get to stay in the castle and we get to stay warm.'

She grabbed her grandmother and hugged her and then, because she was excited, she did a little jig, dragging Maggie round the kitchen with her.

But Maggie had to be dragged. There was no matching excitement in her, and finally Holly stopped and let her go.

'What?'

'There's a catch,' Maggie said flatly. 'There's always a catch.'

'There's not. He's getting a chef and an awesome housekeeper and he's prepared to pay. I was getting those sort of wages in Sydney before…'

'Before you trusted Geoff,' Maggie retorted. 'Have you learned nothing? Men!'

'Gran, he rang the airline and got a real person. And look.' She dug her hand into her greatcoat and hauled out the banknotes. 'This is an advance on what the airline is paying me. It seems you bought me insurance. Gran, this is…'

'Give it back!'

'Are you out of your mind?'

'He's the Earl of Craigenstone. You never, ever trust such a man. We'll be indebted. He'll be demanding… You know what he'll be demanding?'

'Droit de seigneur? Any village maiden he wants?' Holly stared down at the notes in her hand and couldn't suppress a giggle. 'Gran, this is not the Dark Ages. This means dry shoes. And you know, for dry shoes I might even agree to a bit of…'

'Holly!'

'Okay, sorry,' she said, settling again. 'You needn't worry; after Geoff, I am not the least bit interested in unswerving servitude, or even interest, but we do have a job and we can walk away at any time.'

'And this money?'

'Will be repaid as soon as the airline pays me. We're not walking into the lion's den. Come on, Gran, it'll be awesome.'

'How many people are we catering for?'

That stopped Holly in her tracks. She stared at Maggie, who stared straight back.

If they were in front of a mirror they would have seen a weird reflection, Holly thought. Maggie looked like Holly with fifty years added. They looked like two curly-haired Scotswomen, the only difference being the colour of their hair—copper versus grey—a few wrinkles and an Aussie accent versus a broad Scottish burr.

'I don't know,' Holly admitted, hauling her attention back to catering. 'The butler said...'

'Who?'

'The man who opened the door. Dour, lean and mean. He looks like Lurch from the Addams Family.'

'Stanley,' Maggie snapped. 'Estate manager. Reminds me of a ferret. Lurch used to make me laugh. Stanley doesn't.'

'Well, he implied we'll only be cooking and making beds for His Lordship.'

'If he's paying these sort of wages, he'll have invited half of New York.'

'We can cope,' Holly said belligerently and then went back to thinking about the man she'd just left. 'Gran, he's gorgeous.'

'There's no gorgeous about it,' Maggie snapped. 'The man's the Earl, and he's had deceit and tyranny bred into him for generations. I'm glad I'm coming with you, lass, or heaven knows what trouble you'd get into.'

'So you will do it?'

'We don't have much choice,' Maggie said grimly. 'It's follow His Lordship's orders or starve. Nothing's changed in this village for five hundred years, and it seems it's not changing now.'

He made three phone calls. The first was to his mother, who was as upset as he'd thought she might be.

'I'm staying here until after Christmas,' he told her. 'I know how you feel about the place, Mom, but I've told you about these kids. This place is important to them. It's the least I can do. I'll give them Christmas here and then it's done.'

'You won't turn into an Earl?' She'd tried to say

it as a joke but it didn't work. He heard her fear. 'That place traps you.'

'My father trapped you, not the castle,' he told her. 'I will come home after Christmas.' He hesitated. 'Mom, why not come over, too? We could lay a few ghosts. We have an awesome cook and housekeeper. If you don't mind meeting Delia...'

'I don't mind meeting Delia. Contrary to first wife, second wife mores, I don't hate her. She was my only friend in the castle. I understand why she married him and I feel sorry for her, but I still won't come. That place holds nothing but bad memories.'

'Hey, I was born here. Isn't meeting me a good memory?' He was trying to lighten things but she wouldn't be lightened and he hung up with a sigh.

Then he rang his friends and got the opposite reaction.

'You're spending Christmas as an Earl? In a Scottish castle? Awesome! How about making it a party?'

'I'll be looking after kids.'

'But a party!'

He disconnected fast before he found himself with a castle full of American financiers for

Christmas, and then finally he rang the kids. Expecting joy.

But, instead of joy, he was met with silence.

'I almost hoped you wouldn't ring,' Ben said flatly.

To say he was surprised would be an understatement. After the pleading the kid had made on behalf of his family...

'Don't you want to come any more?'

'Yes, but now we can't,' the boy said. 'There's something wrong with Mum's back. The doctor says something's hitting a nerve and she has to go into hospital on Friday for an urgent operation. Gran says Mum can't look after herself afterwards, so we all have to go to Gran's apartment 'cos Gran won't move, and it's even smaller than this one. And I have to sleep with my sisters and there's no one there we know and it'll be the pits. I asked Mum could we go to the castle by ourselves and she said no, not if you're even remotely like our dad, and we looked you up on the Internet and you do look like him and it's hopeless.'

There was a long silence. Angus stared down at the ancient flagstones in the hall and the ragged little dog wound himself round his ankles and looked up at him. Expectantly?

I'm not my father. He didn't say it out loud but he thought it really, really loudly.

'Let me talk to your mum,' he said at last and, moments later, he was talking to Delia. He could hear her wariness—and her weakness and her pain.

'I have a cook and a housekeeper,' he told her. 'If the kids really want to come...'

'I can't let them,' she said and took a deep breath. 'I'm sorry but I don't know a thing about you. I only know you're the Earl and that's hardly a recommendation.'

'But the kids...'

'They'll cope without this reunion Ben's set his heart on. Kids are resilient.'

Yes, Angus thought. This lot had needed to be. And then he thought he'd hired Holly and Maggie for nothing.

'It'd be different if you were married,' Delia was saying. 'If... If I could meet your wife... I just want someone there I can trust. And I hate Stanley. You're not married?'

'No.'

'There you are, then.'

'I'm employing...'

'I don't care who you're employing. No.'

'But I am engaged. My fiancée will be here and she's lovely. Your kids will like her and you can trust her even if you can't trust me.'

What had he just said? The words seemed to have come from nowhere. He didn't think them through; they were just...there. But then he had this vision...

Holly, going down to see this woman. Holly, pleading the kids' cause.

Delia was right, he thought grimly. He looked too much like his father to engender trust, but Holly could talk the leg off an iron pot. Anyone would trust Holly.

If she agreed...

But he'd already said it. What had he done?

'What's her name?' Delia asked, sounding suspicious.

'Holly McIntosh.' What was he doing?

'How do I know what she's like?'

'She's great,' he said warmly. 'Well, I would say that, wouldn't I? I'll need to ask if she'll come down to London to meet you.' He needed to at least concede that. 'But if she's happy to do it, I'll pop her on the train to London the day after tomorrow. If you like her, as I'm sure you will, she could bring the kids back with her. Then you could concentrate on your health. If you're better in time to travel, maybe you and your mother could still join us for Christmas Day.'

There was a sharp intake of breath from the other end of the line. Angus understood it. He was doing sharp intakes of breath all over the place himself.

He'd just landed himself with a fiancée! What had he done?

He'd lied.

But Ben's voice was still echoing. He hadn't been able to deny him.

But what hourly rate would Holly demand for this? He thought of facing her with this new job description, and suddenly he found himself grinning. He might even enjoy the bargaining.

'I never wanted to come back to the castle,' Delia said. 'I only said I would when Ben begged.'

'I can understand that,' Angus said gently. 'But, with Holly here, I think you'll find it a very different place. Holly will make it different.'

'You sound like you love her.' Delia sounded astounded and Angus thought: join the club. *You sound like you love her*? Astounded was too small a word for it.

'And Ben looked you up on the Internet,' Delia

was saying. 'You're not engaged. Or…it says you were, years ago, but your fiancée was killed in a ski accident.'

Delia was sounding suspicious again, and Angus decided, lies or not, engaged or not, it was time to turn back into the aloof financier he was.

'My private life is private,' he said curtly. 'Thankfully, not everything's on the Internet. But, if you agree, I'll have Holly with you the day after tomorrow. No pressure. If you don't like her and trust her then we'll leave it but I think you will.'

'Really?'

'I promise. As long as Holly agrees to come to London.'

And as long as Holly agreed with all the rest.

Holly and Maggie had steak for tea. With chips. With apple pie afterwards. They also had a bottle of wine and then started on another. They'd stoked the fire up, courtesy of Angus's loan, they sat back by the fire after dinner and they grinned at each other like Cheshire Cats. Two well fed, warm Cheshire Cats.

'He'll probably work us into the ground,' Maggie said, trying to sound pessimistic and failing.

'We're both used to hard work and if he works

us too hard we walk out and leave him to it,' Holly retorted and then she thought of the man she'd just left and added, 'but he won't.'

'He's the Earl.'

'He's a nice man.'

'I thought you said there was no such thing as a nice man.'

'Well, a nice person,' Holly conceded.

'But you think he's gorgeous. Every generation there's scandal in that castle because some silly girl thinks the Earl is gorgeous.'

'He's just nice,' Holly said stubbornly, but *gorgeous* did pop into her mind and waft around for a bit.

'We'll see,' Maggie said darkly and poured another glass of wine for them both. Then she giggled. 'I see you and me in the servants' hall for Christmas and I don't see us gnawing on the turkey carcass. I see us carving the best bits for us.'

'Gran!'

'We might even have fun,' Maggie conceded. 'If we can avoid the Earl.' And then she paused.

She needed to pause. The knock on the cottage's thick wooden door reverberated around the living room, imperative, urgent. Maggie frowned. 'It's nine at night. Who… One of the neighbours?'

She half rose but Holly was before her. 'Let me.'

'Take the poker, Holly, love,' Maggie said but Holly, sated with apple pie, wine and heat, was in no mood for axe-murderers. Without the aid of a poker, she opened the door. A blast of snow rushed in, but not as much as she might expect.

The snow was blocked.

On the doorstep stood Maggie's greatest fear. Their new employer. The Earl of Craigenstone himself.

'I'm sorry to disturb you so late at night,' he said, while Holly stared at him stupidly and thought... *What?* 'But I have an additional position to fill and I wondered if you'd add it to your position as cook...as chef.'

'What?' Holly said, thoroughly confused.

'I'm in a bit of trouble,' the Earl said. 'I've made a promise I intend to keep but, to do so...Holly, I need a fiancée. Just for Christmas. I need you, temporarily, to agree to marry me.'

CHAPTER THREE

'I KNEW IT.' The first reaction—of course—didn't come from Holly. It came from Maggie, hissing behind her. 'Didn't I tell you? Talk about a fairy tale. Slam the door in his face, Holly. He's not having his wicked way with you.'

Holly turned and looked at Maggie and then looked at the wine glass in her grandmother's hand. She gently removed it and set it on the hall table.

'Wicked way?'

'He's an Earl.' Maggie glowered.

Holly turned back and looked at Angus in astonishment. He looked embarrassed, she thought. And more. 'He looks cold,' she told her gran.

'Slam the door, Holly,' Maggie demanded again.

'I can't do that. Even if he is crazy, he looks freezing.'

'Holly…'

'He gave me hot chocolate,' Holly said reasonably. 'And enough money to buy us coal. He might be out of his mind but I'm not turfing him out into the night.' She tried to peer through the snow and failed. 'Unless your car's here.'

'I walked,' Angus said. 'It's snowing too hard to trust the road and I needed to walk. I needed to think.'

'So you've given us no choice but to invite you in and warm you up,' Holly said. 'Which we'll do as long as you don't make any more ridiculous propositions. Gran and I have had a bottle and a half of very nice wine and maybe you have, too.'

'I'm sensible,' he said stubbornly and Holly gazed up at him and thought he looked anything but sensible.

Gorgeous was the adjective Maggie had used. *Every generation there's scandal in that castle because some silly girl thinks the Earl is gorgeous.*

But still…

He was wearing the most fabulous man's coat she'd ever seen—thick grey cashmere, tailored to fit. A gorgeous black scarf. Long black boots, moulded to calves that… Okay, don't go there. His after-five shadow was dark, his hair was darker still, and his eyes… They gleamed with what she thought suddenly looked like dangerous mischief and she thought… *Maybe Maggie's right. Maybe I should slam the door.*

But this man had been good to her. This man was saving her Christmas. Maybe a small bit of eccentricity was allowable.

So she ushered him into the living room and she left Maggie in charge in case he needed a strait-jacket and she made them all hot chocolate—no more alcohol for anyone tonight!—while Maggie glowered in the background and Angus filled her tiny living room with his presence.

And with his personality. He was trying to charm Maggie, trying to make her smile while Holly made the chocolate. She watched them through the kitchen door. He wasn't succeeding. Maggie was growing more and more suspicious.

Enough. She took the chocolate in, settled on the edge of a fireside stool—she decided it might be wise not to make herself comfortable—and fixed him with a look that said: *Don't mess with me.*

'Okay, shoot,' she said. 'What are you saying? I'm a chef. Gran's a housekeeper. I thought we had our contract sorted. There was no mention of marriage in anything we spoke about this morning.'

'This is another contract on top of the first,' he said and then added hopefully, 'I'll pay extra.'

'I don't give,' she said carefully, 'extra.'

'No.' He raked long fingers through his jet black hair and Holly realised he looked worried. Really worried. To her astonishment, she found herself softening. 'Of course you don't,' he said, 'but...'

'Tell me the problem,' she said and, to her further astonishment, he did just that, without taking off his coat, cradling his chocolate as she'd cradled hers this morning, seeming suddenly, weirdly vulnerable. He told it all in his lovely growly rumble—the story of three kids who were desperate to come to the castle one last time; three kids whose mother didn't trust him to care for them.

'Is that why you've hired us?' Holly asked in astonishment. 'So we can look after them?'

'I...yes. Or not look after them—their mother was supposed to be coming, too—but I need you to do the cooking and housekeeping so we'll be comfortable. But now Delia's ill and can't come with them. And she doesn't trust me to care for them.' He glanced at Maggie, who was still glowering, and he spread his hands. 'You know my father's reputation,' he told her. 'I can't blame her.'

Maggie was trying to keep stern but this man's charm was seeping through her armour. She was visibly weakening.

'So…you want me to talk to Delia and tell her I'll be responsible for the kids?' Holly asked, trying to sort it in her mind.

'Yes,' he said.

'I can do that, but there's no need for false engagements.'

'There is because I lied. Look….' There went that gesture again, the hair raking. 'I messed this up. I should have spent longer, told her all about you and your gran, tried to reassure her without lies, but she sounded frightened.'

'That's your father's reputation,' Maggie retorted. 'And his father and his father before that. And lying's what they all did.' But still her glower was wavering.

'I know, and that's what I'm up against.' Angus turned to Maggie, sensing the elderly lady's softening. 'I can't fight it but I hoped Holly could. It was a spur of the moment lie but it was made with the best intentions. I thought…if Holly goes to London to see her she can just be…Holly. There'd be no need for deception, except the big one about us being engaged. Holly's a chef from Australia with a gran who lives in the village—Delia knows you, Mrs McIntosh, and once she meets Holly there'll be more reassurance. Holly can be her own bouncy self, but with more control over me and what goes on in my castle than if she was just my chef. Don't you think it might work? Don't you think between us we can give these kids Christmas?'

'Those kids certainly have had a hard time,' Maggie said and, to Holly's astonishment, she was now definitely wavering. 'The old Earl got Delia pregnant and then offered to marry her,' she told Holly. 'I swear it was to avoid paying maintenance. I don't know what Delia was thinking to accept marriage but she did, and she's lived to regret it these last sixteen years. If His Lordship's serious...' She turned to Holly. 'If you can keep your head and be engaged to him...'

'I don't want to be engaged,' Holly gasped. 'I have no intention of being engaged to anyone.'

'It's only for Christmas,' Maggie said, as if she was a bit soft.

'No! You want me to lie?'

'You've been engaged for the last two years.' Maggie seized Holly's hand and held it up so they could see the band of white on her ring finger. 'As far as I know, you haven't even seen the ghastly Geoff since he absconded, so you haven't thrown the ring at him. You can still be officially engaged. Does it matter who to? With luck, you won't even have to lie.'

'You're asking me to put Geoff's engagement ring on again?' Holly was practically speechless.

'No,' Angus said and dug his hand deep into his coat pocket. He pulled out a crimson box and handed it over. 'You'd need this. It's the Craigenstone diamond. My father gave it to my mother and then took it back as soon as they were married—he locked it in the family vault. When my mother left she raided the vault and took it, along with everything else that was legally hers. This has been on every portrait of Craigenstone brides—except Delia—since Time Immemorial. Delia will recognise it. You have no idea of the number of letters my mother has had demanding its return and the satisfaction she had in saying she must have mislaid it. She hates it, though, so there's no harm in giving it away.'

'You're asking Holly to wear the Craigenstone ring?' Maggie gasped as Holly stared down at the extravagant diamond, surrounded by tiny clusters of rubies. Or not so tiny. The size of the diamond made the rubies look small but any one of these rubies would make a ring on its own. The thing was truly over the top.

'I'm not wearing that all Christmas,' Holly gasped. 'As well as all the other objections, what if it ends up in the turkey stuffing?'

'Just while you see Delia.'

'And then you'll lock it back in the vault.'

'That's the one.'

'I'm not taking the train wearing that.' She was looking at it as if it were a scorpion.

'I don't care if it's lost.' He hesitated. 'Holly, that ring's brought trouble to whoever's worn it. Neither my mother or I have fond memories of it. Here's a deal. If you keep this pretence up, if we pull this thing off and give these kids a Christmas to remember, it's yours. My mother and I don't value it and we don't need its worth. It would be our pleasure to give it to you. If it means these kids can have a good Christmas then it'll have gone to a good home.'

'Well, I don't want it,' Holly said with asperity. 'I'd be mugged the minute I went out in public. What use am I to anyone if I'm mugged?'

'Everyone will assume it's paste,' Maggie said soothingly. 'With you looking like you do.'

'That's supposed to make me feel better?'

'That's the other thing,' Angus said. 'We need to get you some clothes.'

'I have clothes and I'm not keeping this ring!'

'We'll discuss keeping the ring later,' he said soothingly. 'If you really don't want it, then we'll work something out but for now it's yours, so if you lose it you don't need to feel guilty.'

'You mean if I'm mugged.'

'Granted,' he said and grinned. 'You can go down feeling virtuous. But you will wear it now, and the clothes question has to be fixed as well. Maggie, where's the most expensive dress shop in town?'

'There isn't one,' Maggie said shortly. 'And you're not sending my granddaughter to London by train with the weather like it is—and not wearing that ring! If you want this done then you do it properly. You take Holly yourself. Can't you…I don't know…hire a helicopter? Isn't that what rich Americans do?'

'Choppers in this weather are more dangerous than cars,' Angus told her. 'At least the trains are still running.'

'But for how long? Trains get stuck in snow-drifts all the time.'

'Maggie…'

'You take her yourself if you want her to go,' Maggie snapped. 'That fancy four-wheel drive you have looks like it'll get through anything; even that pot-holed driveway of yours. And the main road to London will always be clear. There's a great dress shop I've read about in Edinburgh; even royalty goes there. You can stop there on the way. Buy Holly a few expensive dresses. Then you can drive down, flash the ring, persuade Delia to let the kids come and then drive everybody back. Do it properly.'

'Gran!' Holly gasped.

'Properly or not at all,' Maggie said. She folded her arms and glared at Holly and then turned and glared at Angus.

'You're both mad,' Holly said.

'Yes, but I'm rich and mad,' Angus said apologetically, smiling at Maggie. 'And I pay for what I need and I need you. Maybe Maggie's right—it'd be better if I took you to London.'

'I'm hired to cook.'

'With this ring you're hired to be at my beck and call, acting as my fiancée with a bit of cooking on the side. Sharing everything. Except my bed,' he said hastily as he saw her face.

'You'll be a nice old-fashioned couple,' Maggie approved. Then she grinned. 'What a novelty. Do they exist any more?'

'Gran, this is crazy,' Holly gasped. 'It's impossible. The kids will know.'

'Will the kids care enough to think about it?' Maggie demanded, and then added a clincher. 'And think what you could do with the sort of money we're being offered, my girl. Even without the ring... What *we* could do with it...'

That stopped her. Holly's head was whirling but she made herself pause and think. Even without the ring—which she had no intention of keeping—some things were too ridiculous for words. But keeping this job...

They'd earn the rental deposit Gran had no hope of saving for.

That Maggie would be thrown out of her cottage at her age had appalled Holly. Her situation—she had never saved to live anywhere else when she was only renting—was entirely Maggie's fault, Holly conceded, but that didn't make it easier to accept. She'd assumed she'd live in this cottage for ever.

More worldly than her grandmother, Holly had asked the hard question: 'How could you have expected a landlord to let you live in a house for ever?' Maggie had simply burst into tears. There was no answer.

Nor was there a rental deposit.

So, she told herself firmly, start now. This was an engagement of convenience with a salary to make her eyes water. Ridiculous or not, to throw away such an offer would be nuts. Even if it involved wearing a rock. Even if it meant letting this man buy her clothes and drive her to London.

'Fine,' she said weakly. She sounded desperate and she knew it. She took a deep breath though and hauled herself together. 'But…but there are conditions.'

'Conditions?' Angus sounded wary.

'Yes,' she said, thinking of that appalling cold castle and the dust sheets and the horrible Stanley and three kids who sounded as if they needed a decent Christmas even more than she and her Gran did. 'I'll telephone Delia tomorrow morning and talk to her. If she agrees, then we'll go to London on Thursday—you and I together. But tomorrow and Wednesday…

'We'll start at seven tomorrow, won't we, Gran, and we need an open purse. If Gran can find someone else from the village to help us for two days, then I want permission to hire them, too. I want that castle spring-cleaned from stem to stern. I want the whole place warm and I want Christmas decorations everywhere. I want an excellent cooker, hired or bought, I don't mind which, but I do need quality appliances, and I want enough food in stock to make your tummy bulge. It'll cost you a fortune, Lord Craigenstone, almost as much as this ring you're tossing about, but take it or leave it.'

What a nerve, she thought. What an absolute nerve. She'd been tossed a financial lifeline and here she was, putting it at risk. But maybe that risk was necessary. If she was to organise Christmas it'd be a Christmas to remember. The thought of pretending an engagement to a lord in a gloomy, cold ancestral pile made something inside her cringe.

Life had been too appalling. These last months had been hell for her and hell for Maggie. And also maybe for these three kids?

This man before her was their ticket to time out. He was throwing money and rings around with gay abandon. So... One fantastic Christmas before the world closed in again?

'I want a Christmas to remember or no Christmas at all,' she said and met his dark eyes and held them. 'If you're serious about giving these kids a Christmas…I assume the way you're tossing cash about that money is no object.'

He met her gaze calmly, consideringly. 'I pay for value.'

'But if you're anything like your father, you'll hold onto what you pay for,' Maggie interjected. 'You're not keeping my Holly.'

'I'm paying Holly from now until New Year,' he said, still watching Holly. 'I have no intention of staying engaged for one moment longer than I must. This arrangement came out of my mistake—I told a lie on the spur of the moment and I'll pay for it. I'll pay and then I'll move on. I am not like my father. I do not hold.'

'And I have no intention of being held,' Holly said, just as evenly. 'So you can stop worrying, Gran, and start making lists. So, My Lord, do you agree to our terms?'

'Angus,' he snapped.

'My Lord,' she said serenely, 'this Christmas is going to be a fantasy Christmas for all of us. Christmas in Castle Craigie with all the trimmings. I think you should wear your kilt.'

'You want that in the contract, too?'

'Yes,' she said calmly. 'But you're getting off lightly. I could be asking you to dress up as Santa.'

'Not even for you.'

'This isn't for me,' she said without missing a beat. 'This is for three kids and for Gran. That's who I'm doing it for.'

'So you will take my ring?' He held it out again, the outrageous extravagance of it looking incongruous in the extreme in the tiny crofter's cottage.

Holly stared down at it for a long moment. A ring. An engagement ring. She'd sworn...

But this wasn't about engagement. It wasn't even about trust—or not very much. It was about giving three kids a Christmas to remember and giving Gran security. She could do this.

She thought suddenly of what else was demanded—that he drive her to London. It'd mean spending two days in the car with him and a night in London.

'I *could* go by train,' she said dubiously, still looking at the ring.

'No, you can't,' Maggie snapped. 'If you think I want to be stranded alone in that castle with His Lordship while you're stuck in a snowdrift somewhere south of the border you have another think coming. Car or nothing.'

'Is this about you or me?' Holly demanded and, amazingly, her gran chuckled. It was the first time her grandmother had laughed since Holly arrived. Holly knew that laugh; she'd loved it. Every time Gran had visited Australia, which she'd done every year since Holly was born, which possibly explained just why she was so broke now, that chuckle had filled Holly's life. Gran's broad Scottish burr, her laugh, her warmth, her adoration of her son and his wife and their little girl...

It was with her now, all around her, and she knew there was no way she could not do this.

Do it now, she told herself, before you think of any more consequences, and with that she reached forward and took the ring and slipped it on her ring finger.

'Yes,' she said at last. 'Yes, I will.'

'Excellent,' Angus said and smiled. Holly thought: *Don't do that. Don't smile. I can be engaged to you all you like as long as you don't turn on that smile.*

And, as if on cue, his smile faded, as if he, too, sensed danger.

'No strings,' she said, seemingly making no sense at all, but apparently he knew what she was saying. What she was thinking.

'No strings,' he agreed.

'Then that's all right,' she said and turned away

before he could smile again, before she could feel that strong and dangerous tug...

'It has to be all right,' he told them both. Holly knew he was watching her, but she was looking—fiercely—at the ring.

'Excellent,' she managed and, with that, Holly Margaret McIntosh was formally betrothed to Lord Angus McTavish Stuart. For better or for worse.

For Christmas.

CHAPTER FOUR

AT SEVEN THE next morning Stanley arrived to take them to the castle. He barely spoke to them. He was the estate manager escorting the new hired help to his employer. He tossed their belongings into the back of the estate wagon without saying a word.

'As estate manager, he's practically above stairs,' Maggie whispered to Holly as they were transported to their new employment. 'It's a wonder he talks to us at all. As cook and housekeeper, we're definitely beneath his notice.'

But Holly had spent a restless night with a heavy ring on her finger, her unease had been building and this man's covert antagonism had her thinking: upstairs, downstairs—some things had to stop now.

All or nothing.

'We're not the hired help any more,' she whispered, flashing her ring. 'We just got elevated.'

Then she took a deep breath and moved into her newly acquired role.

'How many guests are we expecting for Christmas dinner, Stanley?' she asked from the back seat, where she was wedged with Maggie and Maggie's three large knitting baskets. Holly might only own a handbag and a plastic bag full of charity shop clothing, but Maggie made up for it in the luggage department. Everything she owned she seemed intent on taking, 'in case we need it'.

'How can we possibly need four feather dusters?' Holly had demanded as she'd watched her gran stuff cleaning supplies into Grandpa's old golf bag.

'If you think I'm using what's been lying round the castle for years you have another think coming,' Maggie had said darkly. 'If I were you, I'd be packing a rolling pin.'

'I'll make him buy me a new one if there's not a good one,' Holly had said and Maggie had chuckled again—her chuckle was seeming almost normal now.

'That's the spirit,' she said. 'Ooh, Holly, I think we might be about to have fun.'

But now, as Holly waited for Stanley's answer,

she wasn't so sure and Maggie was looking nervous, too.

'You'll have to ask His Lordship,' Stanley said in a voice that said even thinking of asking would be an impertinence.

'I'm asking you,' Holly said evenly and fingered her ring with resolution.

'It's not my place to tell you,' Stanley snapped.

'As His Lordship's fiancée, I believe I can ask you everything I need to know,' Holly retorted. 'And I believe His Lordship will back up my belief that it's your place to tell me.'

Maggie gasped. There was a deathly silence in the car while Holly rethought what she'd decided last night. That it wasn't enough to tell Delia she was engaged—the engagement would have to be played out the entire time she was at the castle. Otherwise, one phone call would have the kids telling Delia they'd both lied and where would that get them?

She'd expected Angus to have told Stanley the truth. Obviously he hadn't—therefore it was up to Holly to position herself where she needed to be.

'What nonsense is this?' Stanley growled and Holly held up her ring finger so he could see it in the rear-view mirror.

'Love at first sight,' she said sweetly. 'Ask His Lordship. Meanwhile, how many for Christmas dinner?'

There was another silence while Stanley stared at the ring and Holly worried about staying on the road.

'Just His Lordship and the children,' Stanley said at last, sounding so shocked he didn't know what he was saying.

'No friends? No family retainers?'

'No!'

'Well, that makes it easy,' Holly said cheerfully. 'Thank you, Stanley.' Maggie nearly choked but Holly recalled that was just the first barrier. This next three weeks was her gran's future, she thought, and if the fiancée deception was exposed at the first hurdle the whole thing could end in disaster. Therefore, she'd do this properly or not at all.

Bring it on.

And then they rounded the last bend before the castle and His Lordship was standing at the vast doors, waiting, and she thought: *What am I thinking? Bring it on?*

What have I done?

Lord of Castle Craigie. That was what Angus

looked like, even though he'd ditched the kilt. He was wearing casual clothes—cream chinos, an open-necked shirt and a lovely blue, V-necked sweater, rolled up to the sleeves.

He stood at the entrance to his castle home, he looked every inch a Lord, and it was all Holly could do not to jump out of the car and turn tail and run.

She needed to pretend to be engaged to this man?

She must.

The estate wagon pulled to a halt and Angus strode forward to open the doors for them. Nice, Holly thought appreciatively, and she liked it even more that he greeted Gran first.

'Welcome, Mrs McIntosh,' he told her, his dark eyes twinkling. 'I hope you'll be very happy in your new employment.'

'Nice,' Maggie said approvingly, echoing Holly's thoughts. 'Call me Maggie.'

'Maggie,' he said and smiled in a way that made Holly's insides do a back flip. 'And Miss...' he caught himself '...Holly.'

'Hello, darling,' Holly said and wound her arms around his neck and kissed him.

She'd thought this through last night. All or

nothing, she'd thought. Either she was his fiancée or she wasn't.

It had all seemed sensible—last night.

This morning, as she kissed him and felt him
freeze with shock, she thought: *Uh-oh, what do
impertinent cooks get for kissing their Lord and
master?*

Dismissed? Or picked up and carted to His
Lordship's chambers forthwith?

There was a minefield in between.

But she kissed him properly, soundly, as a solid,
assured fiancée would surely kiss her beloved.
His mouth felt strong and warm. His hands fell
instinctively to her waist and held and, for a moment, for just a moment, she let her body believe
this was real, this was true.

Nice? Her body was thinking of better descrip-
tors.

But it was play-acting. Her body had better get
itself in control and tug back. He released her.
Was she imagining it or was there the faintest
hint of reluctance?

Imagination. *Know your place,* she told herself
fiercely. She was a below-stairs employee, paid
to act above-stairs.

'Hello…sweetheart,' the Lord of the Castle managed and she managed a grin in return.

'Very good. We can do this. You might need to do some explaining to Stanley; he's a bit shell-shocked. Okay, show us to our quarters and get this Christmas under way.'

'It's still cold,' Angus warned. 'We won't have heating until I get some tradesmen in.'

'We won't be cold, will we, Gran?' Holly said. 'We have far too much to do. Actually, let's leave Stanley to deal with our bags. If you start with a tour of the castle, we can figure out exactly what needs to be done.'

'Twas like a great man's kitchen without a fire in it.

Where had she heard that analogy? It fitted, Holly thought as Angus led the way through the vast halls and corridors and parlours. But maybe this was worse.

Like a great man's house without a heart in it.

It wasn't just that it was cold—though it was definitely cold. It was that the place was a great stone monument with no attempt made to make it liveable.

'I think I'd rather live in a cave,' she whispered

to Maggie as they followed Angus. Their footsteps echoed on the stone floor—three sets of footsteps: Angus's brisk tread, the soft hush of Holly's dried out trainers and the brisk click of Maggie's sensible low heels. Maggie had appeared all in black this morning, looking very much like a housekeeper in a very reputable establishment. Angus looked the part, too, Holly conceded, casual but still aristocratic. A Lord on his day off.

Holly, on the other hand, felt as if she'd wandered into a movie set and any minute she'd be ejected. She had to put personal feelings aside, she told herself, staring despairingly into yet another dust-sheeted something-room. Even Maggie's shoulders were sagging.

'Show us where the children's bedrooms would have been when they were living here,' she said.

Angus looked doubtful. 'I think I can find it.'

'You think...'

'Stanley showed me through once but I still have trouble figuring out where I am,' he admitted. 'I'm almost up to laying trails of salt behind me so I can retrace my steps.'

But he did find the rooms where Delia and her children had lived and Maggie and Holly stared at them in horror.

They were three bleak rooms off the kitchen. They looked as if they'd been left exactly as they were when they'd moved out. One bedroom with three hard single beds lined up in a row. A smaller bedroom with a single bed—Delia, it seemed, had left the marital bed. A tiny sitting room, four chairs, a table, a threadbare rug.

'You don't need to say it,' Angus said heavily. 'My father was a tyrant.'

'Interested only in money,' Maggie said darkly and then threw a dark look at the current Earl. 'So how come you're prepared to pay us so much?'

'Because I want these kids to have a decent Christmas,' Angus said savagely. 'Like I… Like we never had.'

'You never had decent Christmases in America?' Maggie asked and Holly saw his expression become shuttered.

'We need to make this place more comfortable,' he said tightly and Holly took a deep breath and thought that if she was going to do this—why not do it? She glanced down at the ring on her finger and thought that Angus had just bestowed on her the title of future Lady of the Castle.

Maybe she should do, then, what it seemed previous Ladies of the Castle hadn't been able to do.

This man was an Earl. Rumour was that he was absurdly wealthy. What was a future Lady of the Castle—albeit a temporary one—for, if not to spend His Lordship's money?

'They're not sleeping here,' she said flatly, and Angus and Maggie both looked at her in surprise.

'They're coming for nostalgic reasons,' Angus said. 'They might want their old bedroom.'

'Then we put clean sheets on their beds and leave this room exactly as it is,' Holly said. 'So if they want to use it they can. But they're teenagers, or almost teenagers. Let's give them the teenage fantasy. There must be some vast stately rooms in this place. Why don't we move heaven and earth and give this place—these kids—the send-off they deserve?'

'If they're coming on Friday we can hardly do much,' Angus said, but Holly shook her head in disgust.

'I thought you were an Earl. Can't Earls order stuff?'

'Yes, but...'

'Gran, you know places we can order from?'

'The village won't have...'

'Of course the village won't have,' Holly said. 'Not the stuff we want.'

And then she hesitated. Her heart was warming to the fantasy here. In truth, Holly hadn't had a decent Christmas since her parents had died. Her Australian grandmother had been into austerity, and once Holly started working in restaurants, because she didn't have a family, it always seemed reasonable that she had been rostered on.

Maggie, too… Since Grandpa had died, they'd always phoned each other on Christmas morning. 'Here's another one to get through, Holly, love,' Gran had said every time. 'If I can do it, so can you.'

Another one to get through… Holly thought of those austere beds, of kids in this appalling excuse for a home, and thought: *Why not have a real Christmas? Why not have a Christmas to make up for all the Christmases she'd…they'd missed out on?*

'If you really can afford it,' she said, talking to Angus but almost talking to herself as well, 'I'm talking opulence. Thick carpets by the quarter acre, feather mattresses, pillows by the score. I want light bulbs in all those dusty chandeliers. I want heat and light. Is there somewhere we can hire paintings?' She glanced at the empty walls and then out to the vast corridors behind her. 'We need ancestors.'

'Ancestors,' Angus said faintly.

'Any ancestors will do,' she said blithely. 'And suits of armour and stags' heads, plastic if necessary. I know what a good castle should look like and this isn't one. Maggie, I think we need a bit of help in the dusting department. We'll need electricians and plumbers. Do you know any locals who might…?'

'I know locals who'd love,' Maggie said, staring around her in awe. 'If His Lordship's happy to pay…'

'Um…wait just a minute,' Angus said faintly and Holly put her hands on her hips and fixed him with a stare.

'We're engaged to be married, are we not… dear?' she demanded.

'For three weeks.'

'Then for three weeks I'm the Lady of the Castle,' she retorted, 'and my reputation is at stake. You can just thank heaven you're not leg-shackled for life—imagine what I'd cost you then—but it's all or nothing, My Lord. Make up your mind now.'

'Plastic stags' heads,' he said, even more faintly, and Maggie coughed.

'I think I can find real ones,' she said. 'The Craigenstone Historical Society has about ten stored in their back shed. They might be a bit moth-eaten...'

'We can buy a bit of artificial fur and patch 'em up,' Holly said. 'Excellent.' She hauled a notebook from her pocket and a pencil, and wrote 'Stags' on top. 'Now,' she said happily, 'let's make lists.'

He'd set a whirlwind in motion.

This was no subservient miss. He'd employed a maker of lists.

She drew a map as she went. Every room they went in, she wrote things down.

Two-thirds of the rooms they entered, dust-sheeted seemingly for generations, Holly simply noted as DND on her list.

'Do Not Disturb,' she explained. 'If we take those dust-covers off we might disturb ecosystems that'll have David Attenborough and the Discovery Channel here by lunchtime, and we have enough to do before Christmas, thank you very much. And the kids will love exploring them for themselves.'

But in the rooms she thought they might use—the grandest of the grand—her pen went into overdrive. He stood in the background as she wrote things down and Maggie borrowed his cell phone and started calling.

'My cousin's grandson's an electrician,' Maggie told him while Holly wrote more things on her list. 'He'll be here by lunchtime, and his two sisters are at home for the holidays and would kill for a chance to check out the castle. They're great girls—we'll have this place shiny in no time. As for plumbers, Mrs McConkey's nephew will come and he has a team. Did you know three of your bathrooms are blocked? Were you planning on using one bathroom for all of you?'

Yes, he was. Stanley had already told him— dourly—there was no hope of getting tradesmen by Christmas, and here were Maggie and Holly promising tradesmen by lunchtime.

'Maggie's owed favours everywhere, and with your pay rate it's easy,' Holly said cheerfully. 'We need to move fast, though, if we're to get this done.'

Fast? They were a whirlwind, sweeping through the castle as if it were a two-up, two-down council house. He should leave them to it but it was strangely magnetic. And…Holly was wearing his mother's ring.

What was it about the ring that had him staying around, even interjecting occasionally? He had a mass of work he should be doing—the world's financial markets were still operating and he wasn't here on holiday. He was here to settle his father's affairs, but he'd brought his work with him.

He should…

'Is there anything else you need to be doing?' Holly asked sweetly, and he blinked.

'Pardon?'

'It's just…you're a bit unsettling, hovering.'

'Holly!' Maggie gasped reprovingly, but Holly grinned.

'Well, he is. Don't tell me you don't find him unsettling, too. My Lord, you're our boss. We'll be more productive if you leave us to get on in peace.'

'I thought I was your fiancé,' he growled and she grinned.

'So you are. Well, then, sweetheart, off you go and play some golf or do some other manly thing because we girls want some time together.'

Sweetheart.

'I hate golf,' he said.

'Fish, then,' she said and, to his astonishment,

she reached up, took his shoulders, turned him and steered him towards the door. 'Bye, dear.'

And the door was closed behind him.

Leaving him gobsmacked.

He had a fine housekeeper in New York, an invisible being who did for him while he was at work. He left pay and a bonus at Christmas, but, as far as he was concerned, housework was a mystery.

So why was he feeling as if he wanted to be involved now?

Because one feisty Australian chef was bossing him around?

Because one feisty Australian chef had kissed him?

He could still feel it. The action had jolted him as Angus McTavish Stuart was not known for being jolted. For Angus McTavish Stuart was known for being in control. Hadn't he had control drummed into him from childhood by a bitter, wounded mother?

But then, what man ever listens to his mother? He'd gone his own path—of course he had—and his path had led him to Louise. He'd met her in college, and she'd known about his family money.

Who didn't? But he didn't see the dollar signs in her eyes and he was smitten.

Blond, beautiful, sophisticated, two years older than him, she'd twisted his heart around her beckoning finger, but in the end she was as mercenary as the old Earl had been. She was 'going home for Christmas' she'd told him two months before they were to be married. But home apparently wasn't her parents and her siblings. Home for Louise had been the ski slopes of Aspen, an equally blond ski instructor and the tree that claimed her life when she was drunk after three nights of partying.

The call had come on Christmas Eve. The kid that was Angus had grown up that night. At twenty-one years old he'd stood by Louise's graveside and he'd sworn to follow his mother's mantra for the rest of his life.

Head, not heart. For some reason, that mantra was drumming through his head now.

After one kiss?

This was a pretend engagement for sensible reasons. That was all this was, he told himself harshly as he headed off to find Stanley. Stanley was about to have an apoplexy when he learned what he was proposing spending. Stanley could also blow his story of an engagement out of the water.

For a moment—for just a moment—he toyed with the idea of telling Stanley the engagement was for real, that it was love at first sight, that he'd seen Holly in the snow with her freezing feet and he'd felt an overriding, irrational urge to sweep her up, marry her and live happily ever after.

With moth-eaten stags and lists.

He grinned. Not sensible. Not sensible at all. This mock engagement was a farce.

But...it might be fun, he conceded.

He wanted to join them.

Um...no. He was the Lord of the Castle, he told himself with wry humour. Mingling with the servants was beneath his touch.

But mingling with his fiancée?

Don't go there. Suddenly humour faded.

Head, not heart, he thought savagely in the stillness and then realized he'd only known the woman for a day. Heart? He had to be kidding.

He'd go and talk to Stanley, he told himself. That'd be enough to take the heart right out of him.

Maggie and Holly kept right on taking notes. Their last stop was the most important.

The kitchen.

Angus had briefly opened the door on his initial tour. Now they opened the door wide and Holly stared around her in dismay. Here she'd have to perform a miracle. Christmas cooking. With what?

The kitchen was geared to feed an army—maybe three hundred years ago. The fireplace was vast, open, blackened with age, full of ancient soot and dust, with great black hooks embedded in the stone at either side, where surely a spit had hung, or rods to hold hanging cauldrons.

There was a huge wooden table covered with mouse droppings. The stone floor was filthy, pitted and moulded with age.

There was one cleanish corner holding an old electric stove and a battered cheap microwave oven.

There was a little black dog huddled under the table, about as far under as he could get.

'Hey,' Holly said and bent down and inspected. The little dog backed further. But surely this was the little dog she'd last seen in Angus's study. What was it doing looking so scared?

She headed to the fridge. Obviously His Lordship had been feeding himself. Here were foodstuffs guys thought were important. Eggs, bacon, beer. Not a lot else.

She hauled out a packet of bacon and proffered a bit to the little dog. He inched out, took it gingerly and then backed away again.

She offered more. The little dog inched forward again and finally Holly had him on her lap.

'This guy was in His Lordship's study yesterday,' she told Maggie, frowning. 'He looked fine. Ragged but fine. Now...' She fingered a bruise on his leg that had bled sluggishly. The dog was looking as if he was expecting to be kicked, hard.

'He looks like McAllister's dog,' Maggie said.

'McAllister?'

'He was the gamekeeper here for fifty years. He always had a wee terrier. The last I heard, McAllister was ill and needing to go into some sort of care. We assumed the dog went with him.' Maggie knelt and fingered the little dog's collar. 'It's McAllister's tartan,' she said. 'He must have stayed on with Stanley.' She looked doubtfully at the miserable scrap of canine misery. 'He doesn't look well cared for, though.'

'He doesn't, does he,' Holly said carefully and rose, the little dog in her arms. 'But he was well cared for yesterday. It seems our boss has mood swings. I'll be back, Gran. You make lists on my behalf.' Then she paused and stared at the great fireplace. 'I need a good stove but I need a few other things as well. If we're to work for this guy, we get a contract in writing right now, and this little guy's Christmas is included.'

Angus was having dour words with Stanley. Very dour. The man was driving him nuts, but no one else knew the estate. He had to keep him on, but the sourness of his expression made him want to eject him out of the nearest window.

'You will cooperate with everything Holly and Maggie need,' he said, silky-smooth, in a voice his employees in Manhattan would have quivered to hear. 'Understand me, Stanley, this is non-negotiable.'

'So is this.' And suddenly Holly was standing in the doorway, holding the dog he'd last seen the night before. Blazing indignation. Blazing fury. 'If you kicked this dog, then we're leaving now,' she told Angus in a voice that dripped with contempt. 'Or if you shoved him out in the snow and something else kicked him… Either way, we should walk but I'm giving you two minutes to explain. So explain how the cosy domestic little mutt I cuddled yesterday is now a shivering wreck in your apology for a kitchen.'

'He must have got in the back door,' Stanley muttered, staring at him in distaste. 'He keeps coming back.'

'You lock him out?' Holly was almost speechless. 'Your gamekeeper's dog?'

'He's a stray,' Angus said, crossing swiftly to check the dog for himself. 'According to Stanley, he comes and goes. I only found him a couple of days ago. I need to take him to a shelter.'

'He doesn't come and go,' Holly snapped. 'He comes. Maggie's sure he's McAllister's dog. McAllister worked for the castle for fifty years and you can't even keep his dog?'

'I don't know any McAllister.' Angus took the dog from her arms. The little dog came willingly, as he'd come when he'd found him on the back porch two days ago. 'Where have you been? I went out last night and came back to no dog.' He glanced at the flaming Holly. 'Okay, I know this looks bad but this is a big castle. He seems to know his way round.'

'He's been kicked.'

'I'll take better care of him.'

'How did he get kicked?'

'Holly, this is a stray,' he said gently. 'Yes, I've been feeding him but that's no reason to glare at me like I'm a puppy-murderer. I'm not.'

'Someone is. He's your employee's dog.'

'I'll sort it.'

'You'd better,' she snapped. 'The dog's in the contract. Three weeks' board and keep for him as well. But after this…every single thing we've discussed I want in writing—signed, witnessed, sealed, the lot.'

'Even our engagement?'

She cast a look at Stanley, who was looking—surprise, surprise, dour. 'He knows?'

'That our engagement is temporary, yes.'

'It might be temporary but it's real,' she snapped. 'I'm wearing the ring of the Lady of the Castle and while I'm in charge no puppy will get kicked. He stays with me.'

'In the kitchens?' Stanley asked a trifle too eagerly, and she nodded.

'Yes,' she said. 'And don't even think about notifying the health department. Private residence, my rules apply. And I won't just be in the kitchen; I'll be all over the place, making sure this is a home for Christmas. So get used to it, guys.' She squared her shoulders and met Angus's gaze full-on.

'Sack me now or employ me on my terms,' she said and she lifted the dog back into her arms. 'Decide.'

What was he getting himself into? He was the employer here. Why did it feel the other way around?

And why did she look so cute?

'I'll write the contract,' he said weakly and she gave a brisk nod and headed for the door.

'Fine,' she said. 'Dinner's at seven.'

'I…thank you.'

'For you both?' She glanced disdainfully at Stanley but Angus realised her disdain extended to them both.

Stanley nodded, and she retreated—with dog— leaving him with Stanley.

'She doesn't know her place,' Stanley growled and Angus turned to him and surveyed him from head to toe.

'It seems she doesn't,' he said in that same silky voice. 'But I'm not sure of your place, either. Stanley, tell me all about the dog.'

CHAPTER FIVE

THEY LEFT FOR London late on Thursday morning. The stove had arrived and Holly wasn't leaving until she knew it was installed and working.

There were many things installed and working. All he seemed to have done for the last two days was sign cheques.

To say the castle was a work in progress seemed an understatement. What had seemed an empty, cold mausoleum two days ago was now, to put it mildly, a mess. But it was a warm mess, and it was buzzing with life. They were leaving Maggie in charge and she was in her element.

'You bring those kiddies back tomorrow night and I'll have the place looking more welcoming than my cottage,' she'd assured him, so they left, he and Holly—and dog.

'Because he's not staying behind,' Holly had declared. 'I don't trust Stanley.'

He didn't either but there wasn't much he could do about it. To sack the only person who knew anything about the running of the estate while he was trying to negotiate its sale was unthinkable. Having buyers arrive to see over the estate with the owner unsure even of the boundaries was impossible.

Distrust, therefore, had to be tolerated, even though he was sure Stanley had kicked the dog. He'd be rid of the man soon enough. And he thought that was what Holly had pretty much decided about her boss. She didn't trust him but she was tolerating him.

That should be fine, but it wasn't completely. The dog had soured her view of him and suddenly it seemed important he get that straight.

'I didn't kick him,' he said now as they headed along the road into Craigenstone and turned south, heading for London.

'Either you or Stanley did,' she said. 'But it's okay. He's our dog now. Gran and I will keep him. We're calling him Scruffy for now, because scruffy's what he is. But Gran's going to contact McAllister's nursing home to find out what his real name is.'

'You don't think it'd be a good idea to leave him with Maggie now?'

'She's busy. It'll also do this little guy good to have two days of cuddles. He hasn't had enough.'

'It'll be harder to get a hotel with a dog.'

'I guess you'll need to pay more,' she said bluntly and he winced.

'You don't like me much, do you?'

'I don't know you.' She cuddled the dog some more and wriggled down into the luxurious leather of his four-wheel drive. 'I thought you were nice when I first met you—I even kissed you. But that was when all I knew was that you were giving your half-brother and -sisters Christmas. The dog's reminded me that you don't always get what you see. I'm being careful.'

It was so much an echo of his mother's words—of what Louise had taught him—that it felt weird. Head, not heart? Her mantra, too.

'I would never kick a dog,' he said and she glanced at him and seemed to soften a little.

'Okay,' she said at last. 'Accepted.'

Silence. It felt better, he thought. *Accepted.* This was a woman who said what she meant.

Why was it so important to him that his word was 'accepted'?

'First stop clothes,' he said and she looked dubiously down at her faded, ill-fitting jeans. She hadn't had time to do any more than buy a pair of wellingtons and some knickers at the general store.

'My money hasn't come through.'

'This isn't from your money,' he told her. 'You're presenting yourself as my fiancée. You'll therefore be kitted out as such and it's on me.'

'You must really be rich,' she said, awed, and he cast her a sideways grin.

'Very rich.'

'As in having enough to let us do what we like at the castle and not even blink?'

'That's right.'

'Then why are you selling it?'

'Because I don't want it.'

'Can I ask why not?'

'It made my mother unhappy.'

'Do you want to tell me the story?' she asked, wriggling further down.

She's tired, he thought suddenly. She'd been working flat-out since he'd given her the job and she'd looked exhausted beforehand. She'd been under stress, worried sick, for how long?

Now she was warm, snuggled in his luxurious car, decisions taken out of her hands and he could almost see the strain shift from her shoulders.

He didn't do personal. He didn't tell people his life story, yet here, in this car, in this space, it seemed okay. It seemed part of the warmth. The intimacy?

'My mother was the only child of very rich parents,' he told her. 'She was spoiled, indulged, stubborn and wilful, and she and my grandmother dreamed of her with a British title. My grandfather inherited his money from his very intelligent industrialist father, but he didn't inherit his brains. My grandmother was...socially eager to put it mildly. So the three of them came to London when my mother was nineteen. They met my father, a real live Earl, and they were beside themselves. He wanted her money, of course, so he wooed her with every ounce of charm he possessed. He married her with all pomp and ceremony and then he took her to Castle Craigie. That was when reality set in.'

'Why didn't she take one look and run?'

'Did I tell you she was stubborn? For some crazy reason, the title was still important. She fought and fought with my father, but then she became pregnant. It seemed my father softened a bit towards her then, indulging her a little. But just after I was born Mom's father was diagnosed with cancer. Mom was desperate to go back to the States, but my father turned into the despot that he was. He locked up access to her money, cut communications, hid her passport. I think he must have been a bit mad. Of course she managed it in the end, but the delay meant she didn't get home before her father died. He died at Christmas and she didn't reach her mother until New Year. She's never forgiven my father, or herself for being so stupid.'

'Has she remarried?'

'Are you joking? She does good works.'

'Oh,' Holly said in a small voice. 'Is she…is she happy?'

'I don't think she thinks she deserves happy.'

There was a moment's silence. Then, 'How long ago did this happen?' Holly demanded, sounding shocked.

He gave a rueful smile. 'You know how old I am.'

'Well…' Holly ruminated for a bit, patting the dog. '…that's dumb. Even if she'd fed your father arsenic she might be out of prison by now.'

'You can't force someone to forgive themselves,' he said, trying to sound light, but knowing he was failing. The thought that he'd returned to the castle was bringing sadness flooding back to his mother, and he was feeling guilty because of it.

He'd extended that guilt by inviting three stray kids for Christmas.

'It's ridiculous,' Holly said. 'Totally, weirdly ridiculous. Your mom should have married some other gorgeous hunk—preferably a kind one this time—and got over it.'

'What about you?' Angus asked mildly. 'You've been put through the mill. Are you on the lookout for a gorgeous hunk?'

She cast a fast, suspicious glance at him.

'No! Don't get any ideas.'

'I'm not a gorgeous hunk!'

'In a kilt you are. Whew! But your mother's talking more than thirty years. I'm talking months. I need time to get over my broken heart.'

'And bruised pride.'

'That, too.' She grimaced. 'That makes you safe.'

'Otherwise you'd be launching yourself across the gearstick?'

'Don't kid yourself—My Lord,' she said. 'I've heard your mother's story. I know a moral tale when I hear one and I'm good at learning.'

'So under no circumstances...'

'Under no circumstances. I'm your employee.'

'So you are,' he said and went back to concentrating on driving.

First stop was in Edinburgh, where the smooth-talking lady on the car's navigation gizmo directed them seamlessly to an elegant designer dress store in what Holly guessed was possibly the most discreetly expensive part of the city.

There was a parking spot straight out front. Angus cut the engine and turned to her.

'You want to take my credit card and do this alone?'

'I'm not,' she said, suddenly breathless, 'doing this. I know I can't wear your ring with my ill-fitting jeans and appalling footwear, but don't you guys have chain stores? Big, anonymous shops where I can dive in, buy clean jeans and run. And Angus, honestly, I prefer to do this on my airline insurance. Your card is only necessary until it comes through and I suspect there's not a lot of stuff in this shop I could afford.'

'Let's go see, then, shall we?' He looked almost cheerful, and Holly glowered.

'You fancy playing Sugar Daddy?'

'I never have before,' he said. 'You want to indulge me?'

'No!'

'Then indulge the kids,' he said, smile slipping. 'Their mother doesn't trust me and why would she? If I introduce you and you look like you've bought the cheapest dress you can find...'

'She'll think you're just like your father.'

'That's it,' he said, smiling again. 'So this needs to be part of your role. Prove I'm not my father. Buy expensive, Holly, and let me pay.'

'Just how rich are you?' she demanded and he sighed and sat down in his car again and retrieved his tablet computer from under the seat. He hit the web and a minute later she was looking at an article on the Internet.

Angus Stuart. There was no mention of aristocracy here. There was a brief mention of his grandparents—he obviously came from a lot of money, but that was a mere backdrop.

He'd topped the most prestigious business school in the US. He'd been head-hunted by some of the biggest financial institutions in the world. Under his financial aegis, he'd made small companies big, big companies enormous, and he was now running one of the biggest.

There was a guess at his net worth—once again,

nothing to do with his inheritance in Scotland—
that made Holly gasp.

'That's obscene,' she said, staring at the figure.
'It can't be right.'

'I think they forgot a zero,' he agreed cheerfully.
'But, even if they did and even if that worked
against me, there's still plenty for the odd dress.
Come on, Holly, we're already laying the ghost of
one very miserly Earl. Let's lay it a bit more. You
want me to help or you want to do this alone?'

'Maybe they'd throw me out if I was alone,'
Holly said, staring from the screen to the exquisite window dressing of the shop and back again.
'This is real Cinderella territory, only I get a
longer ball.' She took a deep breath and finally
opened the car door. Instantly a doorman was
beside her and Holly realised the vacant parking
place was specifically designated for customers.

'Would Sir like me to valet park the car?' the
man purred to Angus and Holly thought of her
grandmother sending them here—Maggie was
going to get an earful—and then she looked at
Angus and he was grinning again.

This was a game to him. Maybe it could be a
game to her?

The last few months had been horrific. She still

had debts; she still didn't know their full extent. This was three weeks of time out before horrific took over again.

And this guy was gorgeous. This guy was rich and he wanted to indulge her. This guy was smiling a challenge and she met his gaze and tilted her chin and made herself smile back.

Maybe that was a mistake because smiling at this man…it made her feel…it made her feel…

Nothing. She was allowed to feel nothing, she told herself fiercely. She was acting out a fairy tale and that was all this was—acting.

So get on with it.

'Thank you,' she told the doorman with all the panache a woman in baggy faded jeans could muster as she alighted from the Earl of Craigenstone's car.

Angus sat on a weird Queen Anne chair, which was possibly the most uncomfortable chair he'd ever sat on, while Holly tried on clothes.

From the moment they'd walked into the shop, the manager and shop assistants assumed it was Angus who held the purse strings. Of course they did. He was wearing tailored chinos, a soft cashmere sweater and a butter-soft leather jacket.

Admittedly the dog he was holding looked a bit scruffy, but Angus was dressed to fit in.

Holly was pretty much as he'd first seen her.

Despite his pressure on Holly, he'd had his doubts when they'd pulled up here. But though she still looked like a welfare case, she wasn't abashed.

Australians weren't as class conscious, he thought. She was gazing around appraisingly, as if she had every right to be here.

He introduced himself and explained his fiancée's loss of luggage—his future Ladyship's luggage, he amended, deciding to lay it on thick. They needed everything. The manager beamed and staff appeared from everywhere. He was provided with his chair. Scruffy was provided with a water bowl and a cushion. Holly disappeared into the changing room and came out looking… different.

She was wearing a pair of cream tailored trousers and a classic pastel-blue twinset in yarn so soft you could sense its softness ten feet away. Someone must have produced a comb and settled her unruly mop of copper curls into compliance. They'd powdered her nose and faded her freckles. She looked elegant, she looked expensive—

she looked exactly what the fiancée of the Earl of Craigenstone should look like.

Wasn't that what he wanted? Of course it was, he told himself, and nodded his approval. The manager beamed. 'I think we have one outfit then, My Lord.' He nodded to the assistant who'd helped Holly dress.

But Holly took one look in the full-length mirror and, to everyone's astonishment, she giggled.

'This just needs pearls,' she managed when she stopped chuckling.

Yes, it did, Angus conceded.

'We can arrange that,' the manager said and beckoned for the nearest minion. 'Mary-Anne, slip next door and ask Henry if we can try…'

But, 'I didn't say I wanted pearls,' Holly told him, her smile fading. 'This outfit might need pearls but I don't need this outfit.' She turned to Angus and whirled, showing the full effect of demure and expensive. 'Do you really think this is me?'

'Are we dressing you?' he asked. 'Or dressing a role?'

'I'm not an actor, Angus.'

'What's that supposed to mean?'

'I mean every time I look in the mirror I'll feel

like an imposter. If you want to be engaged to me, no matter for how long, you need to be engaged to *me*. Me. Not what you or Gran or anyone else expects your future wife to look like. Even if I'm acting, I need to put my own stamp on the role.'

The manager looked confused, as well he might. Angus felt confused. Even Scruffy looked a bit confounded.

'You need clothes, Holly. These fit the bill.' These clothes were what he knew. These he understood. They were the clothes of a woman of… quality?

'So you're suggesting two or three more pairs of these trousers, linen shirts like this that I can pop the collar up—Sloane Ranger style—a couple of demure twinsets, a string of pearls, tailored jackets, a little black dress or two, designer flats, court shoes—is that what we're after?'

'Yes,' Angus said definitely, and the manager beamed again.

'We can do that.'

'But I can't,' Holly said and gazed around the shop, and the more she gazed the more depressed she looked. 'I don't see anything red. I like red.'

'We have a sweet little jacket in a very tasteful burgundy,' the manager said. 'It'd look lovely over those trousers.'

'Red,' Holly said with the beginning of belligerence. 'Bright pillar box red. A red that clashes with my hair. Or turquoise green. Or a lovely canary yellow. And I'm sorry but I hate these trousers. I know they're lovely quality but they make me feel like I'm some sort of ageless display item.' She glanced out of the window, across the street. The mannequin in the opposite shop window was wearing a woollen dress, soft purple with diagonal hot pink stripes. 'That's more me.'

'Is that the sort of thing you usually wear?' Angus said faintly, while the manager started to look as if he'd swallowed a lemon.

'No, but it's what I'd like to wear,' she retorted. 'I've spent the last five years saving every cent to buy my restaurant. I wear jeans and T-shirts and my chef's uniform. I work nights so I don't socialise. I have two wedding-and-funeral outfits, one for summer, one for winter, and they're beige because people don't remember beige so you can change a scarf and wear them over and over again. But if you're serious about spending...' She flicked over a price tag and gasped. 'If you're serious about spending *this* sort of money, or, if you're serious about letting me be a fiancée, then I reckon I ought to be *my* sort of fiancée. Does that make sense?'

'Yes,' he said cautiously. 'I think so.'

'But you like this?'

'It's suitable.'

'You haven't exactly chosen a suitable fiancée,' she reminded him.

'I haven't exactly chosen…' But then he looked at the manager's dour face and he decided enough was enough. He wasn't about to discuss temporary engagements in public.

'My mother will probably be coming over… for the wedding,' he told the man consolingly. 'She's American but this style of clothing is exactly what she'd love. That's why I brought Holly here. If I can leave my car here now, I'll bring my mother—and her friends—in for a pre-wedding shop as soon as they get here.'

'Certainly, My Lord,' the man said heavily, casting a look of dislike at His Lord's intended. 'So your mother has taste?'

'Yes, she does,' Angus said and Holly smiled her sympathy at the poor man.

'That's put me in my place properly,' she said and she reached out and took the manager's hand

and shook it with such warmth that the man's disapproval gave way to something that could almost be a smile.

'I'm sorry, but I'm not promising to be a very suitable wife of an Earl,' she told him. 'Right now, I'm a very unsuitable Earl's fiancée. I'm sorry for your trouble. I'd like to say I'll do better, but for now I think you'd better put all your trust in Angus's mom.'

Which explained why an hour later they were back on the London road, with Holly wearing black leggings, blue leather boots that reached above her knees, a gorgeous oversized scarlet turtleneck sweater and a cute scarlet beret that should have screamed at her copper curls but didn't. She had a suitcase of similar clothing in the boot and she looked like a cat who'd finally got herself her canary. Possibly even two canaries.

She'd even managed to find a cute coat for Scruffy and a brand new lead.

He drove and she hugged herself and looked... happy.

How could clothes make you happy? They didn't, he thought. They were a necessity of life, yet Holly kept looking down at her boots and turning her ankles so she could admire them from all sides. Beaming and surreptitiously wiping away imaginary fingerprints.

'My boots are awesome,' she said some fifty miles down the road. 'Thank you.'

'My pleasure.'

'The airline cheque will never cover this.'

'The airline cheque was never meant to. This is your uniform.'

'My uniform would have been the twinset and pearls.'

'It would have made you look more distinguished.'

'I don't think I can do distinguished.'

'You could try.'

'I will try,' she said and polished her boots some more and he thought she looked very, very cute.

The huge ring looked over the top on her finger. It was so big it looked…good.

Suitable for the wife of an Earl?

What was he thinking? He wasn't an Earl, or at least he was but he was already making tentative queries to see if the title could be repealed. He had no wish for any son of his, or grandson or great-grandson, to give himself airs because of outdated British aristocracy. The castle would be sold and he'd be done with it.

The thought gave his mother comfort, relief. Did it do the same for him?

Yes, because he had no wish to be the Earl of Craigenstone.

Even if this girl beside him was to be Lady Craigenstone?

Whoa. What was he thinking? Yes, Holly was cute, bouncy, sweet, but since when had he ever done cute, bouncy, sweet? He liked his women sophisticated, controlled, cool.

'You're being incredibly nice for a dragon Earl,' Holly said, and her words brought him up sharp.

'Dragon Earl?'

'That's what your title's always been. You have a reputation to live up to and so far you're failing. I haven't seen one thing not to like.' And then she blushed, a very cute blush that tinged her whole face pink. 'That is…I didn't mean…'

'It's not exactly a come-on,' he said gravely, 'to tell me I'm not the sort of Earl who bops the villagers with his blunderbuss and throws them in the pond.'

'It wasn't meant to be a come-on.'

'No,' he said gravely. 'Of course not.'

'And you have booked separate rooms for us for tonight?'

'Stanley booked us rooms.'

'Stanley,' she said and he heard disapproval. She snuggled the little dog close and he thought she was still having qualms about what they were doing. 'He doesn't like me, you know. Suppose he tells the kids that we're not really engaged?'

'He won't,' Angus said. He forbore to go further but he could have added that he'd told Stanley he knew about a certain bank account and if he didn't want criminal proceedings then it'd pay him to do what Angus wanted—and be nice to Holly and Maggie.

'Or you'll bop him with your blunderbuss?' Holly enquired.

'You'd better believe it.'

'Ooh, there's the dragon Earl speaking,' Holly said and chuckled again and Angus glanced across at her and it was all he could do not to pull the car to the side of the road, take her in his arms and kiss her.

Huh?

Huh was right. Was he out of his mind? She was his temporary Christmas chef. His pretend fiancée. She was his employee.

He suddenly, urgently, wished she wasn't.

'Do you mind if I use the sound system?' he asked and she blinked.

'Of course not. It's your car. If we try we might find Christmas carols.'

'I downloaded the latest stock market reports that came in overnight,' Angus said repressively. 'I'm concerned about them.'

'Of course you are,' Holly said, changing tack immediately. 'Me, too. And so's Scruffy. You go right ahead and listen and we'll tell you whether you're right to be concerned. I'm no expert, but Scruffy's great at independent analysis. The stock market reports. Let's at them. I imagine the whole world must be worried.'

CHAPTER SIX

ANGUS'S PLAN WAS to drop Holly at Delia's dreary little two-up, two-down and pick her up in half an hour or so. 'Because I look like my father. She'll hate me on sight. It's all my mother can do not to hate me. My presence won't help; it's you who needs to persuade her to let the kids come with us.'

But, 'She needs to trust both of us,' Holly decreed, and in her bright clothes, with her shiny blue boots, she exuded confidence and authority. 'All of us. You and me and Scruffy. We're a team.'

Which might possibly have worked better if the moment the door opened a skinny black cat hadn't taken one look at Scruffy, screeched and headed for the stairs. Holly hadn't been holding the dog tightly enough. He was down and after it, and it took five minutes pacifying to get Scruffy downstairs and the cat down from the curtain rod in the kids' bedroom.

Then they were left with a white-faced, obviously ill woman and dubious kids, the youngest of which—a girl of about ten—was clutching her cat and glaring at Scruffy with disgust.

'Melly doesn't like dogs,' she announced by way of introduction. It was not a good start, Angus thought, but better than the chaos of two minutes ago.

'He's McAllister's dog,' Holly said. She looked at Delia, a woman in her fifties but who looked much older. 'And you're Delia. My grandmother knows you—my Gran is Maggie McIntosh from the village. She says I'm to give you a hug from her but after scaring your cat I'll only hug if you say so.'

It was exactly the right thing to say. The woman's face had been closed, defensive, but both of Holly's pieces of information obviously pierced the armour.

'McAllister,' she said. 'Where is he?'

'He's in a nursing home,' Angus said and Delia glared at him.

'That'd be right. I bet you put him there.'

'I never met the man,' Angus said and Holly subtly moved in front of him.

'Angus might look like your ex-husband,' she said softly. 'But Delia, he's not him. He's been

raised in America and he's only just seen the castle for the first time.'

'McAllister wouldn't go into a nursing home
unless he was forced. And why does his dog look
so skinny?'

'We don't know,' Holly said. 'But we'll find out.'

The woman turned her attention to Holly. By
her side, the children were silent. Waiting for a
verdict? They'd pleaded to come to the castle. In
the face of their mother's dislike, would they still
wish to? Ben, the oldest, a skinny, pale kid who
looked almost malnourished, was looking dismayed at the way this was going. Maybe he was
also dismayed at how closely Angus resembled
his father in person.

He'd begged to come to the castle. Was he now
having doubts? Had they gone to all this trouble
for nothing?

'You're Maggie McIntosh's granddaughter?'
Delia was saying, incredulously.

'Yes, I am.'

'You look like her.'

'Thank you.'

The woman smiled a little, and the tension faded
imperceptibly. 'Maggie was...almost my friend.'

'Maggie believes she is your friend. She says

she definitely would have been if your husband had let her close. She'll be staying at the castle over Christmas as well. She's our Christmas housekeeper.'

'But how did you two ever meet?' She glared again at Angus and took a deep breath, obviously fighting against intrinsic revulsion at his appearance. 'How did you meet...the Earl...if this is the first time he's ever come to the castle?'

'I'm a chef,' Holly said promptly. 'Of international renown.' She glanced down at her bright clothes and grinned. 'I know, I don't look like it, but look at my hands.' She held them out to Delia for inspection and for the first time Angus looked, too. Really looked.

These weren't your normal society miss's hands. They were work-worn hands, hands that had spent years in washing-up water, hands that had come through a long apprenticeship of sharp knives and hot stoves. Her work was on display via her hands and Delia's face softened even further. She reached out and touched them.

'Maggie's granddaughter,' she said wonderingly. 'How...'

'He's eaten my food,' Holly said—which was true, even if it was toasted sandwiches made on the run during the last couple of crazy days. 'And of course when someone said he was the Earl of Craigenstone, how could I not introduce myself and ask if he knew my gran?' She grinned. 'Do you believe in love at first sight?'

'I don't believe in love,' Delia said sharply but she was watching Holly's hands, looking at the great Craigenstone ring, looking doubtful.

Her armour was indeed cracking. She was believing Holly, and suddenly Angus was feeling the magnitude of what he'd asked Holly to do.

Holly was lying for him.

He hadn't asked her to. Well, maybe he had, in asking her to pretend to be engaged, and he ought to have thought that the first thing Delia would ask was how they'd met.

Holly was lying. It felt...huge.

'You're really a chef,' Delia whispered and Holly nodded and handed Scruffy over to the oldest kid.

'You're Ben?' she asked.

'Yeah,' Ben said, and Angus saw conflicting emotions. He still did want to come to the castle, he thought, but he didn't want to hurt his mum.

'And I'm Mary,' the second kid said. Mary, around thirteen, skinny as well, looking more belligerent than Ben. 'I hope you're looking after my badgers. There are so many setts on the estate. McAllister promised to look after them for me. Did you know there's a whole...'

'And I'm Polly,' the ten-year-old interrupted importantly. 'And Melly's my cat. I've only just got her and if Mac's going to chase her then you'll have to *do something*.'

'Mac?'

'I think that's Mac,' Polly said doubtfully, looking at Scruffy. 'But he used to be fatter.'

'Mac,' Mary said, frowning. Up until now, the entire focus of Scruffy had been centred on the cat, but now Mary walked forward and touched Scruffy tentatively on the nose. 'Mac!'

And suddenly the little dog was a wriggling ball of excitement, squirming in Angus's arms until he released him. Mary gathered him up and hugged him and sniffed, and then beamed.

'Mac,' she said emotionally. 'Mac!'

And the tension went out of the air, just like that. Credentials established, via the dog.

'So we have Melly, Polly and Holly for Christmas,' Holly said, grinning and watching Scruffy-Mac try to lick Mary's face. 'And Ben and Mary, plus whoever else is there. Excellent.' She turned to Delia. 'I will take care of them.'

But Delia had more questions—of course she had. 'Is he marrying you because you're a cook?' Delia asked brusquely, turning away from watching Mary and the dog. 'To save him money? Like his father saved money by marrying his housekeeper?'

'He's not saving money and I'm not a cook,' Holly declared stoutly. 'I'm a chef, and I'm *very* expensive. You have no idea how much I've already cost him and continue to cost him.' Her face softened. 'Angus says you're going into hospital tomorrow.'

'I...yes.'

'Do you have plans for tonight's dinner?'

'We're buying takeaway,' Ben said diffidently.

'But we don't like it,' Polly ventured. 'Grandma's coming so it has to be fish and chips 'cos that's all she likes and the cheap place sells soggy chips.'

'You don't like soggy chips?'

'Yuk!'

'Then let me cook dinner for you tonight,' Holly begged. 'For all of you. For all of us. Let me show you how I can cook.' She smiled at Delia—a smile Angus hadn't seen before, a smile that somehow made something twist inside him. 'Let me take care of you tonight as I swear I'll take care of the kids while they're at Castle Craigie. There's no dragon Earl now. There's just me—Holly—my cooking and Christmas, and there's Angus, who doesn't even want to be an Earl. Give us a chance, please.'

How could anyone deny an appeal like that? Angus surely couldn't, and neither could Delia. Holly had wrapped this little family round her little finger by dinner. With dinner.

There was no doubting Holly was a chef. From the get-go they all knew it. Her organisational skills left everyone breathless.

'Right. This is a feast and everyone gets to be included. You tell me your favourite foods and I'll make a list. Your grandma's not here yet but she likes fish and chips? She can't really like soggy chips, though. Anything else? Do you think she might prefer lobster?'

'You can't afford…' Delia started but Angus knew when it was time to step in, so step in he did.

'Cost is no problem,' he said grandly and Delia cast him a surprised look and Holly cast him a grateful look, and it was the grateful look that did that twisting again.

'Cream puffs,' Polly ventured.

'Tacos,' Ben said, looking defiantly at his mother.

'They don't go with fish and chips,' Delia managed but Holly waved objections aside.

'Of course they do. We'll just throw in another course. Delia, what would you like?'

'Chicken soup,' she said breathlessly, still disbelieving. 'I've been wanting home-made chicken soup since they told me I had to have the operation and if you made some… I could put some in the freezer for when I get home.'

'This is looking like a cool menu,' Holly said. 'Mary, what about you?'

'Chocolate pudding,' Mary breathed. 'The kind where the chocolate oozes out. I saw it on telly. Can you make that?'

'Only if we're fast,' Holly said. 'Ben, Angus…'

'Yes?' Angus said, bemused.

'You're on shopping duty. Make a list. Ready?'

'Ready,' Angus managed.

'Right. Write. Go!'

'He really is crazy about you.'

Holly was preparing the mix for the chocolate puddings. Mary and Polly were spooning cream puff mixture onto trays. Delia was sitting beside

Holly at the table. She was peeling potatoes—and watching Holly.

'No Earl that I know ever fell in love with his bride,' she said matter of factly. 'There's always a reason. Angus's father married his mother for money and prestige, and then me for convenience. But you... He can't keep his eyes off you.'

'Then I guess he's marrying me because I wear scarlet sweaters,' she retorted. 'Speaking of which, it's a bit hot. Do you have an apron?'

But Delia was not to be deflected. 'I didn't think Earls could fall in love.'

'My gran says the acorn never falls far from the tree, too,' Holly said. 'But I don't think that's true. I think Angus is a truly nice person.'

'And rich,' Delia said, and Holly chuckled and looked down at the ring.

'And rich. Obscenely rich.'

'I never got a ring,' Delia said and looked at her bare hand.

'Never?'

'Never.'

'Did you divorce?'

'No,' she said. 'It would have cost money.'

'Then you're still married to him,' Holly said slowly.

'He's dead.'

'But you're his widow.' She stared down at the ring and then stared at Delia's arthritic hands. Something twisted. She'd worn a ring for two years and it had meant nothing. This woman had never worn a ring, and something deep inside her told her it could have meant everything.

Behind her, Angus and Ben had arrived back with their load of groceries. How much had they heard? All of it? But Angus was staying silent. She glanced back at her pretend fiancé and his face was impassive.

He'd given this ring to her. It was her wage for pretending to be the Craigenstone bride, and if it was her wage…

She could do whatever she wanted with it.

And what had he said? *If it means these kids can have a good Christmas then it'll have gone to a good home.* Right. If he'd said it, he must mean it. Put your money where your mouth is, Lord Craigenstone, she thought, and gave a fast, determined nod, as if confirming the decision she'd come to. The glance she gave Angus was almost defiant—*stop me if you will, but I know this is right*. She wiped her hands on the dish cloth, and then, before she could have second thoughts—

how much was this ring worth?—she hauled the ring off her finger and handed it over.

'This should be yours,' she said. 'It is yours. Put it on now.'

'Are you…' Delia stared, open-mouthed. Everyone was staring at her open-mouthed, Angus included. 'Are you crazy? You can't. It's yours.'

'It's mine to give,' Holly retorted. 'It's the Craigenstone Bridal ring and, as far as I can see, you're still the Craigenstone bride. From where I'm looking, you haven't had many of the perks of the job. You should keep this one. Angus,' she said, 'I've restored the Craigenstone ring to its rightful owner. You might need to square it with your mother.'

'I can't,' Delia breathed as Angus stared at her as if she'd lost her mind.

'But I'm sure it's the right thing to do,' Holly went on. 'Isn't it, Angus?' She tilted her chin again and met his gaze. Maybe she had no right to make such a gesture, but somehow, seeing Delia, thinking about that great gloomy castle, knowing even a little about what this woman had been through, the thought of wearing this ring herself was preposterous.

'Oh, Mum, it's gorgeous,' Mary breathed.

'Is it really yours?' Ben demanded, and they were all looking at Delia, at a woman worn down by poverty and hard work, who should have been gazing at a ring and seeing how much it was worth in terms of feeding her family but instead was looking at the ring as if it were a gift without price.

'No one treated me like a Craigenstone bride,' she whispered. But then she gazed up at Angus. 'Your father gave this to your mother,' she said, and echoed Holly's thoughts. 'I have no right…'

Uh-oh, Holly thought. Uh-oh, uh-oh, uh-oh. Was she crazy to have made such a gesture? Giving away something that held such history?

Was she out of her mind?

But Angus had said it was hers, and he'd said it in front of witnesses. And now the corners of Angus's mouth were curving into a smile.

'Nice one, bride,' he said and grinned and put his load down on the table. Then he took Delia's twisted, work-worn hands in both of his and held them.

'You have every right,' he said gently. 'I didn't see it until now, but of course Holly's right. You're my father's widow. He treated you abominably. You're ill. We're giving your kids a Christmas to remember, so why not give you one, too? Take this ring, Delia, instead of the equivalent ring my father should have given you years ago.'

'But Holly…' The woman was torn. She looked from Holly to Angus and back again, distracted and distressed. 'You gave it to Holly.'

'It's the Craigenstone ring,' Angus said. 'My mother should have returned it to Craigenstone after the divorce but…'

'But I know why she didn't,' Delia retorted and the faintest of smiles started behind her eyes. 'Oh, My Lord…'

'Angus,' he said sharply. 'You, of all people, shouldn't be using titles. Unless you want me to refer to you as the Dowager Lady Craigenstone.'

'Is that what you are?' Ben and Mary breathed as one.

'Maybe,' Delia said diffidently, and fiddled with the ring. With longing. 'I was a fool to ever think it'd mean anything but I guess I'm still a fool. With this ring…' She took a deep breath, twisted the ring so it settled in its rightful place and then looked at Holly. 'Somehow, with this ring I feel like there was some value in our marriage. That it wasn't a complete sham—that I wasn't a total fool. I know that doesn't make sense, but there it is. Thank you,' she said. 'But you…now you don't have an engagement ring.'

'Then I'll need a replacement,' Holly said happily, and picked up the lid of an empty sauce bottle. 'This'll do. Ben, your next job is to punch a hole in this and round off the edges. Then let Angus check it and he can slip it formally back on my finger. Job's done. Now, doesn't everyone have more jobs to do? Let's get cooking!'

Any lingering doubts as to Holly's cooking ability were laid to rest. She served tiny tacos with guacamole as a starter, then a chicken soup to die for, followed by a seafood banquet which had everyone in the family groaning because there was too much food. But they made a recovery. The irresistible; individual puddings oozed molten chocolate when a spoon broke the crust, with lashings of cream on top. Finally Holly produced coffee and tea and tiny cream puffs that made everyone think they could eat one more thing. Or two. Or even three.

Even Delia's grumpy mother was smiling—smiling too at the ring her daughter was wearing.

'He never gave her anything. Not a thing. And yet here you are…'

'Here we shouldn't be,' Angus said, glancing at his watch. 'You're going into hospital in the morning, Delia.'

'At eight. I'm not allowed to eat after midnight,' Delia said and smiled. 'I think I might manage.'

'Do you have anyone to take you?'

'We'll get a taxi,' Delia's mum said.

'I'll organise a driver,' Angus told her. He hesitated. 'And are you happy for me to take the kids back to the castle?'

'I wasn't,' Delia said. 'But I am now.'

'I'll make sure they phone you every night,' Angus promised. 'And Holly and I will be in touch with the hospital all the time as well.' Then he hesitated. 'Holly…?'

And Holly knew what he was asking. She read it on his face, and she knew it was the right thing. Ben had said Delia would be in hospital for three days and would then be spending her convalescence with her mother. It'd be great if she wasn't worried about her kids. The kids really wanted to come to the castle, but it meant a pretty bleak Christmas for Delia and her mother.

'Of course,' Holly said softly, and Angus gave her a smile that almost made her gasp. But before she could react, he'd turned back to Delia.

'If you're well enough, could I send a car to collect you and your mum for Christmas, too?' he asked. 'We could all care for you.'

'Care,' Delia gasped. 'At Craigenstone?'

'I know, the two words don't seem to go together,' Angus said. 'But Holly's made a difference.'

'She surely has,' Delia breathed. 'Oh, My Lord…'

'Angus,' he said sharply.

'Oh, Angus then,' she breathed. 'Yes, please. And Holly… You're so lucky to have her.'

He was lucky to have her? A woman who gave away a ring that was worth a fortune? Did she know how much it was worth? Could she have guessed?

Did she care?

To say he was blown away would be an understatement. He'd handed her the ring on impulse. It had been a crazy, generous gesture guaranteed to get her cooperation over Christmas. Any woman he'd ever known would have been stunned by such a gift. That Holly, who he knew was in financial extremis, could calmly give it away…

He wasn't angry. How could he be angry—the

ring had been hers to give—but to say he was overwhelmed by the gesture was still putting it mildly.

He'd never known such a woman.

They were quiet in the car on the way to the hotel. In truth, Holly didn't know what to say, where to start. She'd given away the Craigenstone ring.

What was it worth? She couldn't begin to imagine.

'Can you…I don't know…take it out of my wages?' she said at last, feeling swamped. What had possessed her to do such a thing? It hadn't been hers to give. She thought of the debt she already had in her name and she thought, wow, this would see her sink without trace. Cooking in outback mining camps was the best way to make money. That was where she'd be, she guessed, for the next hundred years.

'Do you have any idea of what it's worth?' he asked quite casually, and then, as she said nothing—there seemed nothing to say—he told her.

'We had it insured before I brought it with me,' he said. 'That's base price of the components. At auction it'd go for more.'

She couldn't speak. There were no words.

'My mother will have kittens,' he said.

Silence. More silence as he negotiated the heavy London traffic.

What was she supposed to say?

'Um…you should never have given it to me,' she said and he glanced across at her, his expression unreadable.

'I didn't think you'd value it so little.'

'That I gave it away? It was precisely because I valued it so little. You should never have used it as a bribe. I would have worked for you anyway.'

'Really?'

'You pay pretty good wages,' she managed. 'Without diamonds.' She fell silent again, thinking of the ring, thinking of the number of zeroes, thinking this whole situation was absurd. She hugged Scruffy—or Mac?—because he grounded her. He was her one real thing in this absurd situation.

'Why did you bring it to Scotland?' she asked at last.

'My mother wanted it included in the sale and paid back to the estate. She took it because she knew it'd infuriate my father. She never wanted to make money from it.'

'Well, you certainly won't make money from it

now. I…that was dumb. But it was your own fault,' she said, fighting for a bit of spirit. 'Fancy you giving it to me. What on earth will your mother think?' Her voice faltered a little. 'Will…will you need to tell her?'

'Of course.' He thought about it for a bit and then added: 'Maybe she'll make no complaint. She liked Delia.'

'She liked…'

'Delia was a housemaid during my mother's time. I believe they were friends when my mother needed a friend. The decisions Delia made after my mother left…well, right or wrong, they're past and she's more than paying for them. As for the ring… It paid for itself tonight,' he said softly. 'Good one, Holly. How did you guess how much she needed it?'

'You agree?' she asked, stunned.

'Of course I do. Here I was, waving it round as a bribe and all the time it had a true home waiting. It just took a Holly to find it. Do you know what, Holly McIntosh? You're amazing.'

'I am not,' she said, astounded.

'Don't argue with your boss,' he said and turned to look at her.

They'd stopped at traffic lights, which was just

as well, Holly thought numbly because somehow she met that look. And what followed was one long frisson of something so deep, so powerful, she had no hope of explaining it.

For the look went on and on, as if neither could figure how to break the moment. Finally, tentatively, he reached across and tugged her forward. She found herself leaning into him, closer, closer…

A car honked behind them, and then another. More. A cacophony, reminding them where they were and that the lights were green and they needed to move on.

Angus gave a rueful laugh and tugged away.

'Later,' he said and Holly flinched as reality hit. She backed into her seat and tried to make her racing heart settle. What had just happened? What was she doing? Was she nuts?

'No!'

'No?'

'I'm a pretend fiancée,' she retorted. She held up her weird sauce-bottle ring. 'I'm not a real one. Get over it.'

'We'll fix that in the morning,' he said, glancing at the ring with a smile.

'Oh, for heaven's sake, I'm over rings. This

CHRISTMAS AT THE CASTLE

one's fine. This engagement's for the sake of the children and they helped make this one.'

'You don't want another diamond?'

'This is the third engagement ring I've had,' she reminded him. 'And the last!'

'For ever?'

'You'd better believe it.'

'Holly...'

'No,' she said severely. 'No kissing. No touching. I'm wearing a sauce-bottle ring to remind me that this engagement is a farce. It is a farce, My Lord, and you'd better believe it.'

CHAPTER SEVEN

THE HOTEL WAS over-the-top, breathtakingly gorgeous. Holly sat in the front of Angus's car and stared in awe.

'I've heard of this place,' she breathed. 'I never dreamed...'

'It's as excellent as its name suggests,' Angus said. 'I stay here every time I come to London.'

'Of course you do,' Holly said and then looked doubtfully down at the dog. 'Will they let Scruffy in?'

'Stanley organised it,' he said. 'There won't be a problem.'

There wasn't a problem. Or not much of a problem.

'We've put you in the top floor suite,' the manager told them; he seemed to have sidled from nowhere at their approach to the reception desk, smoothly replacing the girl on duty. 'It has access to our rooftop garden for the wee dog.' He glanced at the wee dog and his face stilled—clearly there were wee dogs and *wee dogs* and this one didn't quite fit his idea of the sort that would fit this establishment.

'Excellent,' Angus said. 'Two bedrooms?'

'One.' The manager frowned. 'Your man did say accommodation for you and your...partner.' He glanced down at Holly's finger and his face froze still more.

'But His Lordship doesn't like sharing with my dog,' Holly said. 'He...he snores. And he smells. He can't help it, but there it is.'

The man gazed at Angus and his expression took a slight turn towards sympathy. It was clear he was wondering how His Lordship had become lumbered with such a crazy duo as Holly and Scruffy. And then he turned apologetic, truly regretful at having to lumber him still more.

'I am sorry, sir,' he said. 'But we don't have room to manoeuvre. Being the last shopping week before Christmas we're fully booked. You have a one-bedroom suite on the top floor. There is a settee. If you like, we can make the settee up into a bed, but...'

'Yes, please,' Holly said and then at the man's look, she tilted her chin. 'I'm an old-fashioned bride,' she said.

'As you wish,' the man said. 'We'll make it up for you, My Lord.'

My Lord. Angus had used this hotel before, but only as Angus Stuart. Stanley had used his title, then. Angus felt his mouth tighten. He'd given orders: make the booking, a suite with two bedrooms, dog-friendly and don't use my title.

Stanley did what he wanted. Stanley had been doing what he wanted for years, he thought. This room was probably his payback for the blast he'd given him for the dog. Still, he was stuck with the man until the castle sold. He was stuck with his dishonesty and his prejudices and his innate dislike of Holly.

But not here he wasn't. Here he had a one-bedroom suite with the woman who was wearing his engagement ring, albeit a very odd engagement ring.

Holly. She looked wonderful. She was wonderful. She was a colourful, warm, vibrant woman who'd just charmed his siblings and his suspicious stepmother.

She was also instinctively retreating.

'Don't even think it,' she muttered as they headed for the lifts.

'What?' He tried to sound innocent but he knew

he'd failed. She glanced at him as if she could read him in neon letters and it was all he could do not to flinch.

'You know very well, so don't even think about thinking about it,' she retorted. 'One errant thought from you and I'm ringing Gran.'

'A worse fate could befall no man.'

'Are you sure you didn't set this up as a one-bedroom?'

'If I'd had nefarious plans I wouldn't have ordered a suite,' he retorted. 'No settee. Though, come to think of it, I always order a suite.'

'Of course you do.'

'There's nothing wrong with being rich.'

'No?' She swivelled to stare at him. 'I wouldn't know.'

'And it's not my fault you're poor.'

She bit her lip at that. They'd reached the bank of lifts. She stood, hugging Scruffy, waiting for the next lift to arrive. Biting her lip some more.

'No,' she said at last. 'It might even be fun to be rich sometimes.'

'Yet you gave the ring away.' He reached out and touched Scruffy, rubbing the little dog behind his ears. He really wanted to reach out and touch Holly but he knew, he just knew, that there was no joy down that road. 'You could have bought a small restaurant with that ring.'

'Wow,' she said, and then the lift arrived and they entered and she leaned against the back and hugged Scruffy and stared straight in front of her.

'Wow,' she said again, more slowly. And then, 'I'm glad I gave it to her, then. Delia should have it.'

'She should,' he agreed gravely. 'But it was a very generous gesture.'

'It should have been made by you,' she said. 'Years ago.'

'I didn't think about it. I didn't know Delia and I didn't understand the situation. But if my mother had given it to Delia years ago, my father would have taken it back.'

'I guess.'

'So you've righted a wrong,' he said. 'Well done, you. But you've done yourself out of a restaurant. Maybe I could help...'

'If you're about to say: let's not use the settee and I'll buy you a restaurant, Scruffy and I are hightailing it out of here right now.'

'Hey,' he said. 'I know you're not that sort of girl.'

'Are you that sort of...Lord?'

'Buying myself village maidens? I don't think I've had enough training,' he retorted and grinned. She looked so cute and so defensive and so... Holly.

But then the lift stopped. The doors swung open and they were in their suite and Holly fell silent. Very silent.

It might only be a one-bedroom suite, but what a suite! Angus had stayed here before, but not like this. Stanley had obviously laid on the title, and maybe also stressed that money was no object, for it seemed they were in the penthouse. The living room was vast. The dining table could seat a dozen, and the windows circling them showed a three-sixty view all over London.

'Oh, my...' Holly popped Scruffy on the floor and did a slow tour, taking everything in. Everything.

For some reason, Angus stayed by the door, watching the girl, watching her reaction.

He was accustomed to luxury—he'd never needed to stay in anything less than a five-star hotel in his life—but Holly...

'This is fantasy stuff,' she breathed. She'd completed her tour and came back to him. 'You have a dressing room that's bigger than my apartment back in Sydney. You have a spa the size of a small swimming pool.'

'We,' he said faintly.

'You,' she snapped. 'Scruffy—and yeah, I know, I should call him Mac but he still feels like Scruffy and he's my security—Scruffy and I are going to haul one of these settees into a corner. Which one makes up into a bed, do you think? We'll then pretend we're peasants. Which, in fact, we are. Angus, your bed…it could take a dozen village maidens.' She grinned suddenly, awe giving way to humour. 'You can have 'em if you like,' she said generously. 'I'll cook 'em breakfast. There's a full kitchen!'

'But I forgot to pack them,' he said mournfully. 'My village maidens.' He gestured to his small valise. 'Socks and jocks is all.'

'And you wouldn't even let the staff carry those up for you,' she said reprovingly. 'Have you no sense of dignity?' She gazed round again and smiled back at him. 'Very nice. Scruffy and I approve. Okay, we're set. You have a bedroom bigger than a football field. Off you go and wallow, village maidens or not, and let Scruffy and I go to sleep.'

'Your bed's not made up yet.'

'The manager said it will be. I'll just…I don't know… I'll try and decide which window to look out of while I wait.'

'You don't want a spa?'

'No!'

'Scared?'

'Yes,' she said repressively. 'And so's Scruffy.'

'There's no need to be,' he said and then he hesitated.

It was not much after nine. He knew she had a gorgeous dress—two gorgeous dresses—in her baggage. He'd watched as she'd chosen them. He could suggest they go downstairs, have a drink, listen to the band, maybe dance…

He knew instinctively she'd refuse.

'Scruffy could do with a walk,' he said, but in answer she unflicked the lock to the nearest door and stepped outside. Here was a rooftop garden, complete with miniature lawn!

'Problem solved.'

'I didn't mean a bathroom walk,' he retorted. 'I meant a proper walk. Besides, it's freezing out there. Anything he managed would freeze midstream. I suggest we put on our big coats and go down to street level. The buildings block the wind. London's full of Christmas. We could do the tourist rubber-necking thing—walk round with our mouths open.'

'I could,' she said and she suddenly sounded a trifle wistful. 'I've never been to London.'

'Then it's compulsory,' he said. 'And now you even have some decent shoes. Coat. Scarf. Hat. Come.'

She hesitated. She really didn't trust him, he thought, and maybe he didn't blame her. He wouldn't trust a lord with his name, and Holly had been hurt before.

He wanted to make that hurt better.

The thought was so sudden and so powerful that it took him by surprise. He watched her hesitation and he thought…

He didn't know what he thought. Only that he was feeling something he'd never felt before. Something he'd never known he could feel.

The urge to reach out and touch her was so huge it was almost overwhelming, yet somehow he held himself back.

Head or heart? Since Louise, head was his mantra, yet here he was, forgetting.

What was he thinking? It was way too soon, too sudden, too inappropriate.

As stupid as falling for Louise?

And thankfully Holly was no longer looking at him. The door had swung open and the bellboy was there with her luggage—courtesy of their shopping, her bags contained a whole lot more than his.

'I bought a cashmere scarf,' she said as the bellboy left, pouncing on it and hauling it from a shopping bag. Suddenly she sounded happy again. This was how Holly was meant to sound, he thought. Happy and laughing and carefree. 'Or, rather, you bought it for me,' she corrected herself. 'I love it. Red and purple and bright, bright yellow. This is just the night to christen it. In honour of your scarf, Lord Angus, let's go for a walk.'

The night was indeed cold. Scruffy wore his brand new tartan coat and his brand new lead. There'd been no snow here, or rain, so the pavements weren't icy. Scruffy was certainly not objecting. He was a gamekeeper's dog, he'd been cooped up all day and he practically pranced along before them.

They weren't the only ones who were out. This was one of London's most popular tourist precincts. Many of the restaurants and shops along the riverfront were still open and there were lots like them, rubber-neckers, tourists taking in the Christmas feel of this great city.

'It's awesome,' Holly whispered as she recognised her first landmark. A drunken party of revellers lurched towards them. Angus steered Holly aside and held her until they passed. They started walking again, but somehow Holly's gloved hand stayed in his. He kept holding and she didn't pull away.

Surely it was an unconscious gesture for both of them, meant to keep them close in the crowds. She'd be a bit nervous, in unfamiliar territory. With the crowds around them, with Christmas lights, buskers, flashing window displays, he'd moved into protective mode and she'd simply accepted what surely must have come naturally.

Surely no big deal, he thought, but the strange feeling around his heart was growing stranger. This was uncharted territory.

This was a gesture of trust...

'Say hello to the lion,' Angus said and Holly stared at an incongruous lion standing sentry to Westminster Bridge. This was a magnificent lion, but...

'Don't look,' Angus told Scruffy. 'You needn't think this is a London fashion. Victorian times called for Victorian measures. This is the Coade Lion and every man in London feels the tragedy that Victorian prudishness has made him sing falsetto.'

Holly choked with laughter and he felt her relax still more. And the feeling around his heart grew…stranger.

They were walking across the bridge now and Holly was silent, taking in the sights and sounds of night-time London. A double-decker bus swept by, one of the many carrying tourists around London. Maybe she'd like a ride.

But then he thought…Christmas. The first time he'd ever come to London he'd walked in on evensong at Westminster Abbey and been blown away by its history and its beauty.

He glanced at his watch. Eleven. There'd be no chance of getting into the Abbey at this hour.

But still he veered towards it because the Abbey itself was enough to take a man's breath away without even going in. As they got closer, as he steered woman and dog towards the entrance, he heard music wafting outwards. It was music to make a man hesitate.

He glanced along the side wall and saw a uniformed security guard.

'Any chance of going in?' he asked and the man shook his head.

'Choir practice, mate,' he said amiably. 'Not open to the public. Unless you're associated with the choir.'

'I'm about to make a donation to the choir,' Angus said. 'A sizeable one. You might mention it to the choir master if you would. And, of course, a tip to you because of Christmas.'

Something slipped between the two men's hands. The security guard glanced down and his eyes widened.

'If you say no, then no it is, but I hope you won't,' Angus continued. 'After all, it's Christmas, the time of giving. I just need you to give me the opportunity to be generous.'

Which explained why, two minutes later, Holly was perched in an ancient pew, leaning against a vast stone pillar in the place where generations of Kings and Queens had been married and buried, where Londoners had worshipped for hundreds of years, and where now a choir of some of what must surely be the finest voices in England were practising Christmas hymns she'd learned as a child. The hymns were so familiar to her that suddenly, here, now, it was Christmas, it was West-minster Abbey and nothing else mattered in the world.

The choir master had beamed them a beatific smile as they'd entered—*what had Angus written on that cheque?*—but now, apart from the choristers, they were alone.

Holly had been running on adrenalin ever since she'd discovered Geoff's betrayal. She'd been trying to figure how to settle debts, to pay overdue wages—to survive in the mess her creep of a fiancé had left her. She'd been gutted by Geoff's dishonesty. Her parents' death had taught her not to trust the world, but she'd trusted again and Geoff had thrown that trust in her face.

Then, when she'd arrived in Craigenstone, she'd discovered her grandmother facing eviction and the sense of desolation and loss had just got worse.

She'd spent the last days working like a Trojan. Today had been just as crazy, but now the world seemed to have stopped to take a breath.

She was seated in a pew whose background made her tremble. Who else had sat here? Angus was right beside her—*right beside her*—in his gorgeous cashmere coat with the slightly suspicious bulge under his arm. That was why he was sitting so close, she told herself. He needed to disguise the bulge that was Scruffy. But the man who'd bustled forth when they'd first entered had been silenced by whatever Angus had put in his hand, the choir master was happy with the cheque Angus has produced, and no one was asking questions.

And the music was all around her, piercing places she'd thought were thoroughly armoured. The choir was singing a layered, magnificent version of *Silent Night*. Her mother had sung this carol to her, and she wouldn't mind betting Maggie had sung it to her father. *Silent Night* was a song for the whole world, and yet here, in this place, it was her song, intensely personal—it was as if they were singing it just for her.

Or maybe they were singing for Angus as well, for his hand was still holding hers. Apart from a little cheque writing, even as they'd smuggled the little dog in, even as he'd held him close under his coat, he hadn't relinquished his grip and she hadn't tugged away.

Why not?

She didn't want to pull away. It was as simple as that. She shivered, but it wasn't from cold or from fear.

It was a shiver of pure sensation. Here in this

night the ghosts were out: Christmas Past and Christmas Present.

It was a shiver caused by their linked hands, and by something deeper, something she didn't understand.

Trust? Could she learn to trust yet again?

What sort of question was that? A crazy question, that was what.

But, lack of trust aside, when Angus dropped their linked hands and put his arm around her waist she didn't object. She couldn't object to anything on this night. Magic was all around them, and for this one amazing time she could forget debts, landlords, thieving fiancés, distrust, a world where fate was precarious, and she could just *be*. She was a woman side by side with a man who took her breath away, in one of the most beautiful places in the world.

They listened and listened and the feeling between them seemed to grow and grow. Within the silence and the music something was forming that she'd never felt before, that she had no hope of understanding. She didn't trust it but she didn't care because, right now, trust wasn't important.

She felt as if she were floating, weirdly, out of

her body but wonderfully, wonderfully, wonderfully.

And then the choir started on the *Hallelujah
Chorus*. This was hardly a rehearsal. This was
the triumph of the night. The voices soared and
the Abbey seemed almost to melt with beauty and
power and, before she could soar through the great
vaulted ceiling, which was what she felt she was
about to do, she made one last desperate attempt
to pull herself together.

'We need to leave,' she whispered, not caring
if he could hear her desperation. 'One minute
more and I'll be on my feet singing with them.'
Or something more drastic. Something she had
no idea about.

'This I have to see.'

'This you don't have to see,' she whispered
fiercely, forcing herself to sound matter-of-fact.
As if this was no special night. No special place.
No special man. 'I have the singing voice of a
tomcat. It's scary. Angus, let's go.'

'Really?'

'The way I'm feeling, I'm about to melt in sheer
awe,' she whispered back. 'I'll ooze down into
these flagstones and merge into all these graves,
which wouldn't be fitting. This is the place for

Kings and Queens and the likes of Charles Darwin. I'm just an Aussie cook.'

'Chef,' he said and she gave a wavering smile but she did manage to pull away, to head out through the vestry—trying not to run, she felt so panicked—leaving Angus to follow if he would.

He did. The security guard nodded to both of them, beaming a goodnight. *How much had Angus given to him?* Angus fell into place by her side, popped Scruffy back down on the pavement and made to take her hand again.

But this time she kept her hand firmly to herself. What had she been thinking? Something had happened in there. Her world had shifted, and she was trying desperately to find even ground again. To make her head work and make sense.

She'd been thinking she could wipe the slate and start again.

Back there, seduced by the place, the music— and the sensation of this man so close to her— she'd been thinking it felt right to be held by the Lord of Castle Craigie. Was she mad?

She'd been thinking the world could right itself—that somehow she could learn to trust. She knew she couldn't, but one more moment of listening to those voices in that place with this man holding her and she wouldn't have been responsible for what happened. A girl had to be sensible.

'Head, not heart,' Angus said and she flashed him a suspicious glance from all of three feet away.

'What?' The comment had come from left field and she veered from determined to confused.

'It's what I've been telling myself for years,' he told her. 'Don't let sentiment hold sway.'

She stopped and stared. It was so much what she had been feeling…so much what she had been telling herself…

'So you were feeling it back there, too.'

'I'm still feeling it,' he said. 'Sensible or not.' He offered his hand again but she looked at it as if it might be a scorpion.

'You're saying head, not heart, but you're also giving in. Ignoring your own advice?'

'I'm suggesting we could take a risk,' he said, and the way he said it…it was as if he was making an effort to keep his voice light. 'The way I'm feeling…maybe the risk is worth it.'

The way I'm feeling… There was enough in that to take a girl's breath away, but a girl had to keep breathing—and had to keep thinking sense.

'I'm over risks,' she managed. 'You gamble

when you have enough to lose without catastrophe. I don't have that luxury. I've gambled before, and I've lost my life savings and more besides. If you think I'm going down that road again...'

'Ah, but we're not talking about gambling,' he said, humour resurfacing. 'Unless I'm mistaken, you don't have any life savings to lose. You just gave away your ring, so how can you gamble without a stake? There's nothing being put on the table here except the way we're both feeling.' He hesitated. 'You are feeling it, aren't you?'

'It was the music.'

'Just the music?'

'Okay, I don't know,' she said honestly, still three feet from him. 'But it's scary to think that it can be anything else.'

'Scary for me, too,' he said. 'I've never fallen for a girl in blue boots before.'

'You can't fall,' she said a little bit desperately. 'I'm your employee and things have changed since peasants followed their lords. Yours is a position of power, and current politics says propositioning me is against the rules.'

'So if I wasn't Lord of Castle Craigie...'

'You are.'

'But if I wasn't,' he said stubbornly, 'you might

consider...I don't know...hand-holding a bit longer?'

'See, there's the problem,' she said, deciding to be honest. They were back on Westminster Bridge. The night was still now, and icy-cold. There were still sightseers veering around them but suddenly they faded—the noise, the Christmas glitz, night-time tourist London. There was simply a man and a woman cocooned by some sort of connection she didn't understand—a connection that isolated them, linked them, held.

She shivered, a racking shiver that had nothing to do with the cold, and he reached out instinctively and touched her face.

She didn't flinch.

'I won't hurt you,' he said gently. 'I'm not Geoff.'

'No,' she said, linked to his gaze. Things were shifting, changing and she felt herself shudder again. She'd been too badly hurt. Too badly betrayed. Her head was screaming at her to step away, that her heart couldn't be trusted, but every instinct was to move forward. To let this man hold her.

'It's too soon,' she managed feebly and he nodded but, instead of withdrawing, he took her hand in his again.

'Of course it is,' he said, gravity fading. 'Much too soon for commitment. If we want to take this further we need a couple of years of careful consideration, lawyers going through the ramifications in triplicate, lots and lots of careful, nit-picking investigation. So let's not.'

'You're holding my hand.'

'Friends can hold hands,' he said. 'They can hold hands while interim ramifications are sorted. Call this preliminary negotiations.'

'O...Okay,' she said cautiously.

'This is friendship by the book,' he said. 'Head, not heart. I have fallen before,' he said gently. 'It ended in disaster. You're not the only one with a broken engagement to your name, but mine ended in death as well as betrayal. So it's hand-holding only.'

'Fine by me,' she said. But was it? She was feeling the warmth of the link between them, the strength—the wonder? But behind the warmth of the link was the shock of his words. She heard the pain behind them, the lesson learned. She didn't need to ask more.

'In a day or two I might stroke your hair,' he was saying lightly, as if to get this back on a normal footing. Slight flirtation, nothing more. 'Just lightly and the agreement is that I provide a comb to fix it afterwards. And I'll let you adjust my tie on Christmas Day.'

'Gee...'

'I know,' he said nobly. 'It sounds too familiar for words but I think we can handle it. It's one small step at a time for the likes of us. Now, let's go home.'

'Back to the hotel,' she said, flustered, because suddenly it seemed important to differentiate between 'home'—personal—and 'hotel'—part of impersonal negotiations within a relationship she didn't understand in the least.

'Hotel,' he agreed cheerfully and swung her arm with their linked hands. 'You're right. Home is something other people do together. Not us.'

CHAPTER EIGHT

ONLY OF COURSE, even though it sounded impersonal, it wasn't. They should have booked two rooms on different sides of the hotel. They were far too close, and Angus was far too large and male and gorgeous, and Holly was warm and full of the sounds of the choir and the wonders of the night and the way Angus had organised things and just...Angus.

The hotel provided hot Christmas punch—the waiter arrived with it steaming, moments after they returned. Without being asked, he flicked on the gas-flamed fire and departed. Fake logs crackled in the fake hearth, and there was some sort of expensive fragrance of pine wafting through the warmth.

It was all too much. Holly was fighting desperately to keep up defences she was starting to doubt she even wanted.

This night... This man.... This moment...

Angus poured the punch and it would have been

surly to refuse, but the moment the warmth hit her stomach she knew she was in trouble.

The glow started from the inside out. Her clothes were too hot for this room. She should strip off her sweater but she wasn't brave enough. She was hardly brave enough to move.

Scruffy had collapsed in a tired heap in the luxurious dog basket the hotel had provided. She needed him, she thought, as the punch warmed places she hadn't known had been cold. She needed to hug him for defence. She needed...any defence she could find.

She was looking out of the great plate glass windows at night-time London sprawling below, and Angus was behind her, watching the sights as well, or maybe watching her; she didn't know and she wasn't about to turn and find out.

'Holly,' he said and the sound of his voice did something to her. Something deep and magical and irresistible.

Head before heart? Whatever their backgrounds, it wasn't working. He was too gorgeous. He was too male. He was too...here.

'Mmm...mmm?'

'Legal considerations seem to be speeding up

faster than expected,' he said softly, and she did turn then and look at him and what she saw...

He was as unsure as she was, she thought. Earl of Craigenstone? No. He was just...Angus. Looking at her gravely. Asking a question with his eyes.

Could she trust?

And more. Something in his expression told her that this was as big a leap for him as it was for her.

Could *he* trust? Could *he* step forward?

Nonsense, she told herself, head trying desperately to get a word in over heart. He's just a guy with a woman in his apartment trying to do what guys the world over would do in this situation.

But... His words came back. *Mine ended in death...* This man was more wounded than she was. This man.

Angus.

'Angus, I'm scared,' she whispered before she could help herself. 'The way I'm feeling...I've just been skyrocketed from a relationship that almost ruined me—a relationship where I trusted far more than I should. I don't think... I can't...'

'You can't kiss me?'

'I want to kiss you,' she said, and her voice held all the longing in the world. 'But you're way out of my league. You're a billionaire American and Lord of Castle Craigie to boot. It scares me.'

'I can understand that.' He took her glass from her hand and laid it on a side table. 'Holly, I'm as unsure as you are. I don't fall for bright chefs in blue boots either, and yes, the way I'm feeling... scared might be a good word for it. But I'm feeling that I need to kiss you. Would that be mutual?'

'No!'

But she was lying. They both knew she was lying. There was that between them... It was intangible but real, as if there was a bubble wrapped around them, not constricting, just gently, wondrously closing in, propelling them closer and closer together.

The fear was receding. The uncertainties. The barriers. One by one they were slipping away into the night.

'Holly...' he said and it was too much—the night, the warmth, the fragrance of Christmas. Or maybe it was more than that. Maybe it was the months of betrayal, where nothing had been what it seemed, where the ground had slipped from under her feet, where foundations had become shifting sand.

And for this man it had been the same.

Angus's hands were held out and the shifting sand was still there, but here, before her, was a link she could take and hold. But she shouldn't. She mustn't. But here he was and the warmth was all around them, and all she did was want.

She wanted so much.

And stupidly, idiotically, irresistibly, she lifted her hands and let him take hers in his. She felt him tug her forward and she felt herself be tugged until her breasts were touching his chest, until she could feel the strength of him enfolding her, the soft brush of his sweater, the heat and strength of his chest underneath.

His breath was on her hair. His hands were tugging her waist, pulling her closer, closer.

She was melting. Fears, reservations, caution, were all disappearing in the magic of this night, this place, this man.

She wrapped her arms around him and she held as well, allowing her body to simply rest on his, his head on her hair, his arms holding her close— her heart transferring to his?

No! That was fantastical nonsense, the stuff of romance novels. This was merely a moment in time, a pre-Christmas weirdness, like kissing your boss in front of the water cooler.

Or not. He didn't feel like her boss. He felt like…Angus.

He was her boss.

So what? her body was screaming at her. Are you going to reject this moment because of your crazy scruples? Are you going to push away this magic?

It would have taken a stronger woman than she'd ever be, because Angus was putting her a little away from him, gazing down at her with those deep, gorgeous, questioning eyes, smiling, just faintly, a smile that said he was as unsure as she was but oh, he wanted…

She knew nothing about this man. Earl of Craigenstone…

She looked at him now and something inside her saw not the Earl of Craigenstone but the remnants of a scarred childhood—rejection from his father, bitterness from his mother, an engagement she knew nothing of except it had ended in disaster, fear of emotional attachment that meant that even now he was looking at her with desire but still she could see the reflection of her own uncertainty.

More. There'd been happy relationships in Holly's past—her parents had loved her to bits, and so had her grandparents. This man, though…

He was flying blind, she thought. He cupped her face in his hands, he gazed down at her and she thought this should be the scenario where the wicked Lord had his way. But this was no wicked Lord. There was only Angus and he wanted to kiss her and all she had to do was allow those gorgeous, wondrous hands to tilt her chin...

And of course she did. How could she not? He was here, he was now, he was her gorgeous Liege Lord, but he was her man besides. Her knees seemed to be giving way beneath her, as did her principles, as did her fears.

There was only Angus. There was only this moment.

She lifted her hand and traced the contours of his face, as if she had to know him, she had to feel every inch of him, and with every fragment of touch the feeling went further.

He was gazing gravely down, waiting, waiting and she knew there'd be no compulsion. No would mean no. But yes...

Yes was out there, filling the room, making her heels suddenly lift from the floor so she was on her toes. So he could draw her in and enfold her to him, so she could finally, wondrously allow his mouth to meet hers...

So he could kiss her as she ached to be kissed.

She could finally be where she needed to be.

Oh, the kiss...

She knew kisses. Of course she knew kisses. She was a woman who'd been engaged, who knew her way around in the world, who knew men.

She didn't know this man. She didn't know this kiss.

It was a fusing of two opposing charges. It was heat and power and promise. It was a surge of something that rocked her almost from her feet, that made her tilt those heels higher, that made her melt, sink into him, take as he was taking.

That made her want...

She wanted this man as she'd never wanted anything more in her life. But maybe that wasn't true. *Want* was too small a word.

It was as if her mouth had located her true north and was holding. This was her true course. This was her man.

Her body was hard against his, her breasts crushed against his chest and she could feel his racing heart. Hers was racing in response. The world was shifting, lighting, colours appearing that she'd never known before, shards of sensation rushing through that she'd never felt, never thought she could feel.

But now wasn't the time to question anything; now was simply for letting this power take over her body, opening her mouth, allowing her man to deepen the kiss, demanding that she too could take the taste of him, the feel of him…

Her man. Her Lord? Her Angus.

They were by the great plate glass windows, the lights of London were all around them and, if London cared to gaze upward, two star-crossed lovers were silhouetted against the penthouse windows of one of the finest hotels in the city and it looked like magic. For Christmas magic happened…

But then…how old had Holly been when she'd realised Santa was a fairy tale? How had she felt when reality finally broke in, as break in it must?

As break in it did, now.

She'd been tugging him close but she wanted him closer. She shifted to hold him tighter, to mould her breasts against his chest…and her makeshift ring caught in the wool of his sweater.

Such a tiny thing, and a different woman might have tugged and torn and not cared, but his sweater was gorgeous cashmere and she'd been hugged against it and she loved it and the thought of ripping it felt like hurting him.

So she froze so she didn't hurt it further—and the kiss broke. He loosed her a little to see what was wrong.

'I'm stuck to your sweater,' she managed. Her voice didn't work properly. Nothing was working properly. 'My ring...'

'Leave it.'

'Let me unhook it.'

'It can stay hooked,' he growled, gathering her tight again. 'It's an engagement ring. Isn't that for bonding two people together? Isn't that where we're headed right now?'

She stilled. She let the words echo in her head, and with that echo she felt cold, hard sense shove its way in.

Bonding two people together...

What was she thinking? How long was it since she'd ripped off Geoff's ring? How long was it since she'd thought she was...bonded?

'No!' The word broke from her lips before she even knew she was going to say it. 'No!'

No? Of course no.

He heard her panic and he replayed his words,

and in that fraction of a moment he knew they'd been the stupidest words he could have used. Here he was with a woman he hardly knew and he was talking of tying her to him. When he knew her background… When he knew her fears…

Was he out of his mind?

'Let me…let me unhook it,' she was saying, or she was trying to say it but her voice had changed. She'd changed.

There was nothing for it but to relax his hold and then, as she was still stuck, he hauled his sweater over his head and moved away still further.

Her ring and her finger were still inside his sweater. He was no longer attached.

He felt…empty.

'Tug the ring off so we can fix it,' he told her, but she shook her head, her expression shuttered. Something inside had recoiled and it was staying that way.

'I'm keeping the ring on,' she told him. 'I made a deal. I've given Delia your ring and I'll wear this one for three weeks but it doesn't bond me to anything.'

'Of course not. But love…'

'*I am not your love.*' She practically yelled it, then turned away, twisting the sweater inside out,

as if it was desperately important to unhook herself even from his sweater. 'Of all the crazy set-
ups… What were we thinking?'

'I know what I was thinking.'

'No! Angus, I'm on the rebound. I'm not ready.
And I don't think you really want…'

'I do really want,' he said, trying to gather his
wits. Knowing he needed to step back but it was
almost killing him to do so. 'But I can wait. Holly,
how long does it take to unhook a ring?'

'You'll need to wait longer than that,' she said
savagely. 'Lord or not.'

'Can you cut it out with the title?' And suddenly more than Holly's past was in the room
between them. His ghosts were all around them.
His words were an explosion, his anger coming
from nowhere. 'Holly, I'll wait for as long as you
need to wait,' he told her. 'But this will only work
if you think about me and not my ancestry. *I am
not my father.*'

And that was another dumb thing to say. He
raked his hair in disbelief that this had suddenly
changed so appallingly. He met her gaze and he
saw fear. He'd shouted. Of all the idiots, he'd
shouted.

Appalling was too mild a word for it.

Where had the ghost of his father come from? He felt ill.

'Holly, I'm sorry,' he said, trying to get a handle on what had suddenly become a situation she looked as if she wanted to run from. He had to wipe the fear from her face. Concentrate only on that, he told himself. Nothing more.

Step back. Step right back.

'What I just said was dumb,' he said at last. 'No, I'm not my father, but you already know that. What I am is your boss.' Deep breath. 'Holly, I've employed you for three weeks. After that, I won't be anything to do with any inherited title and you won't be my employee. It'll also be that much further from Geoff's treatment of you. My father's my ghost and Geoff's yours but we can be free. Holly, believe me, I'm not holding you to me now, and I won't hold you to me then, but I can wait and see what happens—when we're both free.'

She didn't answer. She didn't even look at him. Stupidly she was still trying to untangle the sweater.

He should help her but he daren't approach. He could still sense her fear.

Three weeks. Such a short time to lay ghosts...

But, until the New Year, she'd be living in his castle. The thought was good.

'We both should step away,' he managed. 'Tonight's been great but we're both obviously tired. Right now, I'm not making sense even to myself. So let's both go to bed—with a door closed between us.'

She nodded, still clutching the sweater. 'Yes.'

'Holly...'

'Doors. Boundaries. We need them,' she said dully. 'Goodnight... My Lord.'

'Please don't call me that.'

'It's what you are.'

'Until I sell,' he conceded. 'But after that I'll be living in the US and I am not My Lord there. This fantasy will be over.'

'Good, then. Excellent.' Her face was set, expressionless, as if she was carefully hiding her emotions. 'Tonight's been part of that fantasy,' she said. 'And fantasy knows its place, so let's move past it. It's more than time we went to our separate beds.'

'Holly...'

'Forget the personal,' she managed and finally handed him his untangled sweater. 'You're my employer so forget the kiss. Think of me as hired

help, a sauce bottle ring, paid for in cash fiancée.'
She held out her finally freed, beringed finger.
'I need to bash out a few rough edges but that's
what I am. Angus...'

'Yes?'

'Go to bed,' she said gently. 'Because I really, really want to kiss you again but it's just as well my
ring saved the day. This is an impossible situation
and we both need to keep our heads. If you're the
least bit interested in kissing me when I'm done
being your servant and your fiancée then you can
think about propositioning me again, but by then
hopefully I'll have my head together. We've both
been stupid. Kissing's done. Go to bed.'

He went to bed but he didn't sleep. He lay and
stared at the ceiling and watched the flickering
lights from the city play over the plaster. Eventually he rose and stared out over the river. He
poured himself a whisky and then tossed it down.

There was a tentative scratch on the door, low
down. Dog. He opened it a fraction. Holly was
through there and he wouldn't wake her. Scruffy
padded through, jumped on his bed and looked
at him as if he was expecting night-time confi-
dences.

With the door safely closed, it was safe enough to talk to the dog.

'I want her,' he said simply and Scruffy kept on gazing at him as if more was expected, more was to come.

It was hard to resist a dog with his head cocked to one side, especially when the words were already in his head.

'I'm not pushing her,' he said into the silence. 'I don't take and hold. I'm not like my father.'

For some reason he was remembering his eighth birthday. His grandmother had given him a piggy bank, a weird-looking pig that grunted when a coin was dropped on its tongue before it proceeded to 'devour' the coin. He'd loved it. He'd also loved the bright coins his grandmother had given him to go with it.

'You could use your money to buy ice skates,' his mother had told him but he'd shaken his head and proceeded solemnly to feed his money to his pig.

Maybe he'd thought he could get it out later. Maybe he hadn't even wanted ice skates. No matter, the next thing he'd known, his mother was sobbing.

'He'll be just like his father,' she'd told his grandmother. 'I know it.'

And then, when he'd decided to study finance...

'How can you be interested in money? You are just like him.'

And finally, when he'd fallen for Louise...

'How do you know you love her? You just want her, isn't that right?' And appallingly, as grief and humiliation had given way to insight, he was left wondering whether she was right.

Just like his father... His mother seemed to have softened over the years, she let him be, but the old accusations were always there to haunt him.

Enough. It was more than time to be over the past, he told himself. Right now, Scruffy was eying him sideways, as if there was something deep he didn't understand. It was as if the little dog was saying: *The most gorgeous woman you've ever met is right through that door and you're on this side thinking about past history. Are you mad?*

This dog had brains.

Maybe he was mad. Maybe they both were. If they could shake off the past, Holly would be lying in his arms right now, skin against skin, her lovely body moulded to his, her warmth, her breath against his lips, her hands…

'Cold shower,' he told Scruffy and Scruffy looked at him again as if he were crazy.

'I might well be,' he told him. 'But sometimes a cold shower is sensible. Believe it or not.'

Scruffy didn't believe him. He knew it.

He didn't believe it himself, or part of him did but the other part was telling him his feet were heading for the bathroom when they should be heading for the door to the sitting room.

'Sense prevails,' he muttered savagely. 'How do I know the difference between wanting and loving? I can't, and I will not take advantage of an employee.'

'So sack her,' he demanded of himself.

'Yeah, right. That's what your father would do. Go take a shower.'

She'd heard the door open, just slightly, and she'd held her breath.

She'd heard Scruffy wuffle through, she'd heard Angus's soft greeting and she'd heard the door close again.

She heard Angus head to the shower.

She lay and listened to the muffled sound of

running water and she tried, really hard, not to imagine the Lord of Castle Craigie as he was now. Naked under running water. Rivulets of water running over a body she just knew would turn a girl's knees to water. That jet-black hair dripping, water running over his face, his shoulders, his chest, down...

'You're a sad case,' she told herself and hauled her bedclothes over her head to block out as much sound as she could, and tried and failed to block out the images being conjured.

Why was he taking a shower now, an hour after they'd gone to bed?

A cold shower?

That brought more images and a girl could almost groan if she didn't think that maybe the walls were too thin and a girl shouldn't do anything of the kind.

She'd sort of like a cold shower herself. Or a good brisk walk in the snow, but it was the wee hours in a strange city and a girl had some sense.

But sense was in short supply. If her ring hadn't caught... If Angus hadn't made that crack about bonding...

That kiss had melted sense entirely. If Angus had wanted her tonight she would have...

Yeah, well, let's not go there, she told herself. Sense had prevailed and it was just as well.

And sense would stay prevailing. She knew that now, somehow, things had been put on the right footing. For the next three weeks she was chef and pretend fiancée and that was it. Then she'd take her money and run.

Fast.

CHAPTER NINE

THINGS WERE STRAINED between them the next morning, but okay. They could do this. They had to do this because the kids were waiting.

They found the kids packed and excited, but torn about leaving their mum. A limousine was ready to take Delia and her mother to hospital as soon as they left. Delia was tearful but determined to let the children go.

'I never would have let them if I hadn't met you,' she told Holly. 'I can't believe His Lordship is marrying someone so lovely.' She gazed down at the Craigenstone ring, still blazing on her finger. 'I'll get Mum to wear this while I'm in hospital and it'll give her pleasure as well. I can't believe you've been so generous.'

'It's Angus who's generous,' Holly told her. 'If he hadn't agreed I never could have done it.'

Delia eyed Angus dubiously. He was busy stowing baggage and cat-carrier into the back of the car, and explaining to Scruffy why the cat was out of bounds. They had space to talk, and suddenly it seemed as if Delia had the courage to probe.

'So…you love him?' Delia asked.

Holly hesitated, twisting the weird little tin ring on her finger. She was supposed to be this man's fiancée. Her lie had to continue. 'I guess I must,' she said. She watched Angus some more and thought…maybe I'm not lying. Heaven help me, maybe I'm not.

'If you're not sure…you be careful,' Delia said urgently. 'It's not my place to say, but oh, my dear, the Craigenstone men can be charming when they want something. Charming and ruthless.'

But if he'd been ruthless he could have had her last night, Holly thought, as finally they waved goodbye to Delia and set off northwards. He hadn't pushed. He'd respected her suddenly imposed boundaries. So far, she hadn't seen a hint of ruthlessness.

Though she had seen more than a hint of charming.

She was about to see more. They'd barely crossed the Scottish border when Angus turned off the motorway.

'Quick deviation,' he told them. The kids were being amazingly quiet, amazingly subdued in the back seat. They'd been told by their mother to stay subdued, Holly thought. They must have been for this wasn't normal. They'd stopped an hour back for lunch, there'd been little conversation then and there was no protest now.

Agree to everything—was that what Delia had told them? Was that the way she'd tried to deal with the old Lord?

She eyed Angus and tried to figure just how ruthless this man could be. He was rich in his own right. You didn't get rich by being a doormat.

He wasn't a doormat, but ruthless? The word stayed with her, a question. She'd accepted Geoff without nearly enough questions. She was asking questions now.

Why? He had no intention of coming near her for three weeks. After that, he'd be back in the States and she'd be in Australia. There was no need for questions.

But the way she was feeling...

He glanced across and met her gaze and smiled and something inside her melted, as it had melted before. Oh, help, this was nuts. This was teenage crush territory.

Was this why the Earls of Craigenstone had

been deemed dangerous for generation after generation? All they had to do was smile.

'I thought we'd pay a visit to my father's old keeper, McAllister,' he said. 'Maggie found out where he is—in a nursing home not far from here. I thought he might like a visit from Scruffy.'

And she melted again, just like that. Ruthless? Ha!

She glanced down at her crazy ring and she thought that if it had been a bit less rough she might have spent the next three weeks *really* pretending to be a fiancée.

And where would that have left her? She was in an emotional mess already. Would she break her heart over Angus as well as Geoff?

She hadn't actually broken her heart over Geoff. He'd smashed her pride, he'd humiliated her to her socks, but had she felt for him what she was feeling for Angus?

No! No, because she wasn't feeling anything for Angus except sheer, unadulterated lust. It must be lust. The man was exuding more testosterone than any man had a right to and it was doing things to her insides…

'Do you have a comb?' he asked and it was as much as she could do to get her voice to work.

'Wh...why?'

'Scruffy's going to meet his master,' he said. 'He might like to look his best.'

If she'd felt emotional before, what happened next almost wiped her.

The kids stayed outside. They knew McAllister but they reached the foyer, smelled the unmistakable smell of hospital-type institutions and backed away like alarmed colts.

'Don't you like McAllister?' Angus asked and Ben nodded.

'He was...great. But he won't be now, will he?'

'So you're sending us in as forward reconnaissance?' Angus asked, grinning, and Holly's heart did that crazy twist again.

'He won't want to see me,' Holly ventured. 'I'm not part of this. It's you who's Earl of Craigenstone.'

'Yes, but you're my fiancée and it's your job to support me.'

'Angus...'

'Yes...dear?'

'Fine,' she said and girded internal loins and tucked a gleaming Scruffy—or as gleaming as

Scruffy was ever likely to get—under her arm and headed inside with Angus.

The nurse at reception eyed Scruffy askance but she wasn't given a chance to object.

'We've brought Mr McAllister's dog to pay him a Christmas visit,' Angus said and smiled at her and the girl was no more impervious to that smile than Holly was. Of course she nodded, of course she smiled back and she led them down to a lounge area where a dozen very old persons were desultorily watching television.

She gestured to a *very* old man in the corner. 'There he is. Dougal, you have a visitor.'

The old man was slumped in something that looked a cross between a wheelchair and a bed. He was wearing an ancient tartan sweater, grubby trousers and a tweed cap that looked as if it was welded to his head. It'd have to be stuck there because the old man's head hung so low his chin reached his chest. He didn't look up when his name was called. He didn't move.

Oh, help. No wonder Scruffy—or Mac?—had been left behind, Holly thought. This man looked as if he'd been old for ever. Was it even worth trying to get through to him? Unconsciously, her arms tightened around Scruffy, as if to protect him from seeing his master in such a state, but Angus was made from sterner stuff than she was. He took Scruffy from her, strode across the room and squatted before the old man in the wheelchair.

'Dougal,' he said, and then more firmly, 'Dougal!'

The man's head lifted fractionally but it was definitely a lift and it was enough for Angus to gently insinuate one little dog onto the man's knees, under that bowed head.

He lifted one of McAllister's hands and laid it on Scruffy's head. 'This is your visitor,' he said firmly, loudly enough to be heard across the blaring television. 'We've brought him all the way from Castle Craigie to see you, so you might as well say hello. The kids say his name is Mac. Is that right?'

There was a moment's stillness, from dog and from man. The focus of the room was no longer on the television. One of the residents leaned forward and hit the remote and the sound of the soap they were watching died.

Scruffy was perched where he'd been put, on McAllister's knees. The little dog stared upward and McAllister's hand moved, as if involuntarily, to hold...

But he couldn't hold for suddenly the strange smells and sounds and place faded to nothing as a light bulb switched on in the little dog's head. From where Holly stood she could see the second he realised... This man who was holding him...

McAllister! McAllister! His total, obvious joy exploded, upward and outward.

But it was as if he knew the old man was fragile. He was going nuts, but gently nuts. He was writhing upward, his entire body trembling with shock and excitement, pressing closer, licking the old man's chin, practically turning inside out with delirious joy but gently, gently, not one scratch...

And now the old man had done his own recognising. His hands were holding, hugging, and his age-lined face was practically collapsing in on itself. He hugged the little dog close—or as close as a wriggling, whimpering, licking bundle of canine ecstasy could be hugged—and tears started tracking down the wrinkled cheeks.

'Mac,' he said brokenly in a voice that sounded like rasping gravel. 'Mac, boy, you've found me.'

The whole room was watching them now. There were sniffs from all while they watched the greeting, a long, lovely ode to devotion past. There was no hurry. They were taking their time, these two, two old mates back to being one.

'That's...that's the first word I've heard him say for six months,' the nurse behind Holly said, and Holly turned and handed her a tissue. She'd just fished a handful of them out of her bag. She wasn't sharing many, though—she needed them herself.

'How long has Mr McAllister been here?' Angus asked and there was an edge of steel in his voice that Holly was starting to recognise.

'Eighteen months,' the nurse said. 'I'd just started working here when he came in. Apparently he had a stroke at work. He was in hospital for weeks and this was the only place that had a long-term vacancy. He came by ambulance; he's never had a visitor but about a week after he arrived a guy who said he was the manager of the place he worked dumped a whole lot of his stuff here.'

'A man called Stanley?'

'I'd have to check.'

'He has no other visitors?'

'No.'

'Can he keep his dog here?'

'No.' But the girl had lost her efficiency and

was sounding human—and apologetic. 'I'm so sorry but he can't. The owner doesn't allow any pets, even visiting. I'm breaking rules letting you in here.' She smiled an apology. 'But I'll let you keep breaking them for a while. Some things are worth it.'

'Can we take him out into the garden?' Angus asked and two minutes later they were wheeling a wrapped-up Dougal and dog outside.

The kids were there. They stared at Dougal with horror—this stroke-affected old man was obviously a very different Dougal to the one they remembered—and then Ben finally found the courage to talk.

'D...Dougal. Do you remember us? I'm Ben.'

'O...of course,' the old voice whispered. 'Ben, lad. Eh, where've you been?'

'London,' Ben said and it was like removing a cork from a bottle; the voices were freed and suddenly all three kids were talking at once, clustered round the chair-cum-bed, and Angus and Holly were on the outside, watching.

'We can't stay long,' Holly whispered, still clutching her tissues. 'Not if we're to get back to the castle before dinner. Oh, but Angus...'

'Are you any good at nursing?' he demanded and she looked at him as if he'd lost his mind.

'What?'

'Nursing? If not, is Maggie? Either one of you?'

'As a nurse I make a very good chef,' she said, suddenly seeing where his thoughts were taking him. 'Angus, I can't. I'd love to but I'm your chef and your fiancée for Christmas. I can't be anything else.'

'If we all helped...'

'He's so frail.'

'But if we could have him for Christmas. I don't know anything about nursing either, but Holly...'

'Just how many people,' she said carefully, 'are you thinking of inviting?'

'It's a very big castle, and I have employed someone who's said to be an excellent chef.'

'I'll feed him but that's all I'm capable of. And Angus, wouldn't it be cruel? To take him and then bring him back here?'

'He's not coming back here,' Angus said, grimly determined. 'I'll find him somewhere better. Somewhere he can keep Scru...Mac.'

'Oh, Angus.'

'But first, Christmas.' He turned and walked back to the entrance with Holly, leaving Dougal in the garden with the kids. The nurse who'd greeted them was standing in the doorway.

'Problem,' he said. 'We want to take Dougal home for Christmas but we need a nurse.'

'A private nurse,' she said cautiously. 'I don't know...'

'For the right person, I'll pay twice the going rate,' he said. 'Plus accommodation, in Castle Craigie. Plus all the Christmas trimmings.'

'Really?'

'Really.'

'That'd be fantastic,' the girl said, and suddenly she sounded wistful. 'And Dougal's a sweetie.' There was a couple of moments silence while they saw her doing internal calculations.

'I've got my holidays,' she said at last. 'But my mum's alone and we have Christmas together.' Her face was suddenly kind of hopeful. 'My...my dad died last year. It's going to be a bleak Christmas. But Mum used to be a nurse, too. Dougal's very frail. He could do with two nurses.'

'Expanda job,' Angus said. 'Why didn't I see that coming?'

'Sorry?'

'No. The more, the merrier,' he said, and suddenly he was grinning. Holly looked at him, startled. He had the attitude of a man about to toss pound notes to the masses. 'When do your holidays start?'

'Next F-Friday.'

'Then what if I send a car—or do I need to hire some sort of ambulance? Can you organise that? Yes? And of course I'm paying your mum, too. Now, let's go make sure Dougal wants to come, and see if he has any aunts or mothers or cats or wolfhounds that he'd like to put on my payroll as well.'

He was a very nice man.

He was her employer.

He was gorgeous.

Tucked back in the car, cuddling Scruffy-cum-Mac, Holly felt herself near to tears. Of all the impulsive, crazy gestures… Dougal had wept when Angus outlined his plans, and Holly had felt the need to steer Angus out of there before any other solitary geriatric had crossed his path.

'Our castle's filling up,' she said.

'I'm going to wear my kilt.' He sounded deeply contented and she cast an amazed gaze at him.

'You sound smug.'

'As soon as I saw that wardrobe full of kilts I knew I wanted one Christmas as Liege Lord.'

'What's Liege Lord?'

'I'm not sure but it sounds important. I bet it involves sitting at the head of that vast dining room table with an epergne with tiger heads in the middle, and slicing the Christmas turkey with a ceremonial sword.

'Maybe two turkeys,' she said.

'We Lords can handle two turkeys.'

'Why don't you want to be a full-time Lord?' she asked curiously. 'Why the rush to sell?' The tensions of the night before were still with them, she could feel them, but somehow what had just happened had made her relax a little.

'I belong in the US.'

'If your home is your castle, then you belong here.'

'Ask my mother whether that holds true,' he said, humour fading. 'She's appalled I'm here now.'

'Why don't you invite her as well?'

'What, my mother?'

'Everyone else is coming,' she said. She was feeling...how to describe the way she was feeling? She was heading back to a castle with her boss, with a car full of kids and dog, with the kids' mother and grandmother, aged retainer and nurse and a nurse's mother following. Punch-drunk might describe it.

Kissed might describe it as well.

'As…as long as you made sure she knows the engagement is pretend,' she added, feeling even more disoriented, but more and more thinking that if the castle was to be full, why not make it really full?

For some reason, what had happened with Delia and with Dougal was shifting perspective past the personal. She and Maggie had been heading for a bleak and solitary Christmas. It would be anything but solitary now, and somewhere this man's mother was living with ghosts and it seemed as if they were making her solitary as well.

Her relationship with this man was causing tension, but she could get over that. Hopefully. And more people, more to do, would help.

'She'd have a pretty good idea as soon as she saw that ring,' Angus said, guy-like, focusing on practicalities. 'I need to do something about it.'

'Tell everyone you're waiting for the after-Christmas sales before you buy one,' she told him.

'As the Earl of Craigenstone, that's entirely believable.'

'It is, isn't it?' he said and suddenly his voice was savage and the tension was back. The kids were dozing in the back seat, listening to their music on a sound system that could thankfully be muffled in the front. It had been a long drive. There was now less than an hour to go, and it seemed as if they were cocooned in the front of the car, with nobody to hear them, with a weird sense of connection that might have everything to do with the kiss of the night before. 'Holly, you don't want my mother here and she's already said she won't come. She loathed the place.'

'Did she loathe the place or loathe your father?'

'Same...'

'It's not the same,' she said stubbornly. 'Gran and I will make this Christmas stupendous. We're intending to lay ghosts all over the place.'

'Let's have Hogmanay,' a sleepy voice said from the back seat. 'Then it's not just Christmas. We can have Christmas and then at New Year we can have a party for everyone and say goodbye to the castle and everyone in the whole village.'

'What's Hogmanay?' Angus and Holly said as one.

'New Year!' Ben's voice was incredulous. 'Don't you guys know anything? In Scotland Hogmanay's bigger than Christmas. It's a goodbye to the old year, in with the new. Other big landholders hold parties for everyone on the estate. I told our father that once and he just snarled, but it'd be so cool to do it. With a bonfire and everything.'

'Hey, fun,' Holly said.

'Hey, wait for my snarl,' Angus retorted, but he was grinning. 'So you want most of the world to come for Christmas and everyone left over to come for Hogmanay?'

'Yes,' Holly and Ben said in unison.

'If this road wasn't icy I'd throw my hands up in the air,' Angus retorted. 'I thought I was Liege Lord, in charge of all I survey.'

'The peasants are revolting,' Holly said smugly and Angus glanced over at her, seeing her smile, the cheery wink she was giving Ben, the flush in her cheeks and the gleam of excitement at the challenge ahead and he thought…he thought…

He thought the peasants weren't revolting at all. And one peasant was so far removed from revolting that every piece of personal armour he'd ever loaded himself with was in danger of disintegrating into dust.

But he wouldn't invite his mother again. The thought of her, in her Christmas black, with her Christmas grief and her accusations… No. That was the real world. This was a pretend Christmas, nothing to do with reality.

Maggie had had two days and two girls from the village to help, and Maggie and two girls—plus her tame electrician and plumber—were a force to be reckoned with. As they rounded the sweeping driveway and the long grey fortress-type castle came into view—it was covered with fairy lights.

Covered with fairy lights.

It was just dusk. There was a collective intake of breath. Angus even stopped the car.

'What…?' he breathed.

'You…you did say to do whatever was needed to make these kids welcome,' Holly managed, looking at the fairy lights, looking at the castle and thinking how much it had cost her to string one row of fairy lights across her apartment entrance last year.

'Wow,' Mary breathed from the back seat. 'It's a fairy castle.'

'It's your home for Christmas,' Angus said,

managing to recover. 'Welcome back to Castle Craigie.'

And the shocks didn't stop there. They walked into the hall and the first impression was warmth. The second was sheer, over the top Christmas.

There was a Christmas tree standing in the vast baronial hall, and it wasn't just a Christmas tree, it was practically a full-grown pine. It was decorated with what must be every conceivable ornament Maggie had been able to drum up—no tasteful colour coordination here—and it glittered on a scale that took every single one of their breaths away.

Except Scruffy-cum-Mac. Holly put him down, he headed straight for the base of the tree—and Holly had to race across and grab him before he could raise his leg.

'Welcome home, My Lord.' Maggie was at the head of the stairs, dressed in severe housekeeping black, and Holly had to bite back a giggle. Maggie was part Gran, part housekeeper, part actress and she was filling her role to perfection. 'And these are the children of the castle. Welcome back, Misses and Sir. Can I show you to your bedrooms?'

Maggie turned and trod stately upward, the actress in her in full swing. The kids stared after her in awe, they followed tentatively—and then, from where they stood, Holly and Angus heard gasps of wonder, awe, incredulity. It seemed that Maggie had decorated a bedroom for each of them in the main part of the castle, and in the style that each of them had never dreamed of.

'I've got two suits of armour in my room,' Ben yelled out to his sisters. 'Wow! Wait until I tell my mates on Facebook.'

Holly giggled and then glanced up at the man beside her and her giggle died.

He was looking...grim.

Grim? Why?

'What's with the face?' she asked, and she saw him physically brace and shift and his smile came back on.

'Face?'

'Like Scrooge seeing Tiny Tim's tiny corpse because he didn't share his turkey.'

'I'm sharing.'

'For this Christmas only?' she asked curiously. 'Do you usually share?'

'I don't usually need to share.'

'Need? Or want?'

'There's no need to get personal.'

'No, but there's want,' she said, suddenly, impertinently, wishing to dig a little deeper into the past of this enigmatic Lord. She glanced at her weird ring. 'As a fiancée, I need to understand my true love.'

'Your pretend true love.'

'Oi,' she said. 'You want me to shout to the top of the Christmas tree that this engagement's fake? These kids will go home. Maggie and I will head off in a huff. You'll be left with McAllister and Stanley. If we're engaged, then I get to pry a little. Why does the sight of a Christmas tree and whooping kids make you look like you've just swallowed lemons?'

'Lemons!'

'Lemons,' she said definitely. 'Give.'

What was it with this woman? No one in his extended circle of friends and acquaintances would push past his personal boundaries like this.

'I don't do Christmas,' he said at last, and she stared at him as if he were out of his mind.

'Um…it's a bit late to tell us that now,' she managed. 'You've opened the castle, you've invited the hordes, and I have two turkeys, two puddings and the ingredients for every conceivable Christmas goodie in the pantry. Plus Gran already has

Christmas plans afoot, and the kids are already planning Hogmanay.'

'I know.'

'So why…?'

'My fiancée died on Christmas Eve.'

'I accept that,' she said thoughtfully. 'I can see that must have been devastating. But wasn't that a long time ago?'

'Yes,' he admitted. 'But then we hadn't been into Christmas when I was a child either. My grandfather died at Christmas.'

'That's right,' she said thoughtfully. 'Was he old?'

'Seventy-two.'

'Okay, then,' she said. 'Got it.'

'You don't "got it".'

'No,' she admitted. 'I don't got it. Tell me.'

Tell her? Why? And how? It was dumb, how such a long ago tragedy still affected his life. He'd never talked about it, but every Christmas there it was—his mother deep in mourning while the rest of the world seemed to burst with flashing lights and colour.

His mother still wore black on Christmas Day. Actually, she wore black every day.

'You can't stop grief,' he said but the explanation sounded weak even to him.

'No, but you can keep it to yourself. Your mother...'

'Holly, she's over it. I'm over it. It's just background.'

'But it still makes you purse your lips at Christmas decorations.'

'I do not purse.'

'You do so purse.' She sighed and put her hands on her hips. 'Okay, you're over it. Prove it. As Christmas host, it's your duty to enjoy Christmas, starting now. Come into the kitchen and help me make mince pies.'

'I can't cook!'

'Of course you can. If you can handle the stock market you can handle a recipe, and what else are you going to do? The kids will be exploring old haunts, and with all these people I've invited I could use a kitchen hand.'

'I'm not,' he said cautiously, 'a kitchen hand.'

'No. You're a fiancé with a big black hole where Christmas should be,' she said blithely. 'I intend to fill it. I have Christmas carols on my phone and I have a beaut little travel amplifier that can boom them through the kitchen. I intend to sing along. How can you resist that, Lord Angus?'

He couldn't. He knew he couldn't.

He didn't.

Holly McIntosh was a sucker for heroes. Any hero. Give her a good romantic movie and she'd fall every time. The only time a movie got her really upset was when a perfectly good hero ended badly. Ooh, the end of *Butch Cassidy and the Sundance Kid,* where two perfectly good heroes went down together, still had her smarting at the waste.

She carried her heroes in her heart for months after seeing an excellent movie, and she didn't let anything mess with her images.

The Lord of Castle Craigie was a hero. She'd decided it the moment she'd met him. Those dark, shadowed eyes, the sculpted face, the fact that the first time she'd met him he was in a kilt, with his castle, his haunted background... Yep, she was in meltdown and *that kiss* had just compounded things. If her ring hadn't snagged at just the wrong moment she knew she'd have gone to bed with him and made love to her very own romantic hero.

And yet...and yet...

Suddenly tonight the hero image had slipped a bit. The image wasn't tarnished, it was just that she was seeing the human bits underneath more clearly. The Lord of Castle Craigie as a solitary child, spending Christmas with a grieving mother who never let her son escape a past which, in truth, was nothing to do with him. And then some kind of no-good fiancée dying on Christmas Eve. Okay, she knew nothing about the long-dead Louise, but right now she was prepared to put her in the same category as Geoff. Low life.

Because she'd hurt her hero?

She was kneading one lot of biscuit pastry while Angus—under her supervision—was crumbing butter into flour ready for the next batch. Her fingers were required for kneading but what her fingers really wanted to do was curl into frustrated fists. His mother… His fiancée… They were both in her sights.

What a way to treat a child, she thought, glancing at his still set face, but then, what a way for the old Earl to treat his wife. She might judge the unknown Louise, but maybe she needed to cut Angus's mother some slack. To be locked in this castle while her dad was dying, for no better reason than a crazy sense of control, would probably have damaged anyone.

'Angus, why not push your mother to come?' she urged again. This was none of her business. She had no right to urge, but to have ghosts perpetually in the shadows... 'How can she let ghosts ruin her Christmas for ever? If she's miserable, I can tell that you won't enjoy yourself. Her ghosts are your ghosts. Bring her here and let us blast them out of the water with mince pies and mistletoe. If she'll come, let's show her that life can go on.'

'She wears black,' Angus said inconsequentially.

'Black's elegant—it'll look stunning among all our glitz. She'll match Maggie. Honestly, Angus, if you don't invite her you'll regret it. I can see by your face that you'll be thinking of her all Christmas.'

'What could I possibly say that'd make her come?'

'Tell her you really are engaged,' she said. 'Tell her you've given me the heirloom ring but I seem to have lost it already. Tell her I'm adorable and cute and dumb and you've fallen hard and you're thinking of getting married on Hogmanay. You've

invited all the villagers to attend and you're be-
sotted. Make me sound like a gold-digger. I suspect there's not a mother in the known world who
won't get on a plane with that impetus.'

'You're joking.'

'You can't pull it off?'

He thought of his mother's reaction if he really
did say those things. And then…he thought of his
mother's Christmas.

It wasn't that she was deliberately playing Miss
Havisham, he thought. It was just that she'd got
herself into a roller coaster where Christmas every
year was the bottom of her ride.

Even the top wasn't very high, he thought, and
he looked at Holly in her crimson apron with Father Christmas emblazoned on the front, and her
bright blue boots—she'd hardly taken them off—
and he thought this Christmas Holly would cheer
anyone up.

Maybe he could lay a few ghosts, he thought.
If he could get his mother here… Underneath the
layers of sadness, maybe there was a grandma in
the making.

Grandma. Um…he was moving ahead here.
Grandchildren.

Children.

He'd never thought of having children, except as some vague, nebulous concept he might or might not expect in his future. But suddenly his future was here, now, standing before him, elbows deep in pastry, eying him with a distinct challenge.

'Christmas is for family,' she said. 'I was desperate this year so I headed to Gran. You guys sound like you've been desperate every year, so why not head here? We'll have fun.'

Fun at Christmas. The concept was alien.

Holly. She was almost alien as well, as far from his world as it was possible to be.

Christmas. Hogmanay. Castle Craigie.

'That mixture's crumbed enough,' Holly said, hauling him back to the here and now. 'Give it to me and start another.'

'How many mince pies are we making?' he demanded, startled, and she grinned.

'How many mince pies does your mother eat? I've just added another batch to my list. But think about it, Angus—Christmas, holiday, Hogmanay, family—wow this is a year to celebrate.'

'I thought you just lost your real fiancé—plus all your money?'

'So I did,' she said serenely. 'Deep down, I'm a

bucketload of misery, but misery likes mince pies just as much as anyone else.'

Misery had got herself thoroughly, totally distracted. Misery had almost forgotten to be miserable.

Every now and then a wash of remembrance would flood back—of her cute little apartment in Sydney, now in the hands of the receivers, the staff she'd had to let go, her humiliation at the hands of a man she'd thought she could trust with her life. But mostly she was just too busy to care. She had the Christmas to end all Christmases to prepare for, and then Hogmanay.

'Hogmanay is huge on most of the big Scottish estates,' Maggie told her. 'It's always been a source of sadness that the old Lord wouldn't do it. Now you've talked this Lord round your little finger...'

'I have not!'

'You have, even if you won't go there,' Maggie said serenely. 'And this year marks the end of the estate as we know it. Somehow, we seem to have gained permission to put on the feast to end all feasts, so let's get this celebration planned.'

And in the slivers of time not spent cooking and planning, when Holly could lie in bed and stare at the ceiling and think of Geoff and his betrayal, another face intruded.

The Lord of Castle Craigie. A man who, astonishingly, was throwing his heart into the festivities to come and was trying his utmost to show three needy kids a very good time.

This afternoon they'd headed off on the estate tractor to find a yule log. 'I'll order one if you really need one,' Stanley had said sourly, but Angus and the kids had ignored him and headed for the woods.

'Come with us, Holly,' the kids had pleaded. 'Don't you want her with us, Angus? She can't spend all her time in the kitchen.'

Angus had looked at her with a quizzical smile and she could have gone—she could—only sense was still there, yelling in her ears, saying: *get to know this man better first.*

And then they'd brought back the yule log, a great lump of green timber that would no sooner light than fly, and Maggie had decreed another was needed, and Maggie would personally select the log, so off they'd set again and once more Holly had stayed behind.

Fingering her odd little ring and feeling an ache in her heart grow deeper.

Why had he employed her to cook when he wanted to be with her? He and his assorted tribe headed off into the snow for the second time, with Maggie giving instructions as to where the rotten wood would be, the kids whooping behind or cadging an occasional lift on the running boards and Scruffy-Mac perched on his knee and he thought—the only thing needed to make this perfect was Holly.

He'd seen the longing on her face as they'd set off. She wanted to be with him.

No. Um…she wanted to be with *them*. There was a difference.

But…but…

How long did it take a man to know his own heart?

No time at all, he thought as they rounded the bend in the drive and the castle was out of sight. She'd return to her kitchen, they'd get back in an hour or so and the whole castle would be filled with the results of her cooking.

And she'd smile as they walked in. As he walked in.

A man could come home to that smile for the rest of his life.

How would she fit in Manhattan?

She didn't have parents. As far as he knew, she had no unbreakable ties to Australia, and Maggie had to leave her cottage. If he asked Maggie to join them…

'Left!' Maggie was perched behind him on the tractor. 'That's the third time I said it. Any further and we'll be in the loch.'

'Sorry,' he said and veered left towards the woodlands. 'Maggie, have you ever been to New York?'

'No.'

'Would you like to go?'

'Why would I want to go to New York? No one would understand my accent.'

'Everyone would love your accent.'

'What exactly are you proposing?' she demanded.

'Nothing yet,' he admitted. 'It's just…if I ever thought…of proposing…for real…'

'Give her time,' Maggie said sharply. 'She's still raw.'

'I know that.' He hesitated. 'How much time?'

'How would I know?' Maggie demanded. 'My Rory wrote to his mother the day he met me, saying he'd met his bride. While he was doing that, I took my best friend Jean to look at wedding dresses in the most expensive bridal boutique in Glasgow. But I've heard tell that other people take their time to make up their minds, and I do think Holly needs time. It's just I have no idea how long. And she needs to be sure. After all, you're the Lord of Castle Craigie and, knowing that, a girl would need to be very sure indeed.'

My Rory wrote to his mother the day he met me, saying he'd met his bride.

Maggie's words stayed in his head as he played with the kids, joining in a snow fight, losing more of his dignity all the time. He'd become Angus. He was becoming almost a friend to his half-brother and -sisters and, to his astonishment, he found he was enjoying himself—a lot. Family. He'd hardly had one and now it was a strangely sweet sensation. Making the kids happy. Making them smile, and having them make him smile back.

But family... Was that why Maggie's words stayed with him?

My Rory wrote to his mother the day he met me, saying he'd met his bride.

Her words mixed with the crazy conversation he'd had with Holly over the mince pies—and finally that night he cracked and phoned his mother.

'I think you should come for Christmas,' he told her on the long distance call. 'There's someone I need you to meet.'

'Who?' He heard his mother's sharp intake of breath, followed by unmistakable fear. She'd be frantic the castle was having its own effect on him.

'A girl called Holly,' he told her. 'She's...extraordinary.'

'Angus! You've been there for less than a month.'

'And I've known Holly for less than a week. Time's immaterial. Mom, I've given her your ring.'

'You've what? After a week? Are you out of your mind?'

He was following Holly's instructions to the letter and it was working. He could feel his mother's fear; the same thing that had happened to her was happening to him. It'd work. She'd be over here so fast, to rescue her son from some harpy's clutches...

But suddenly that didn't seem such a good idea. *Make me sound like a gold-digger.* That was Holly's order and if he did it, yes it'd work, but at what cost?

He did not want his mother to think his Holly was a gold-digger.

His Holly? He stood staring out into the snow-filled night and he felt his world shifting. One slip of a girl, one mince pie maker, one changer of worlds.

Family.

'She gave it away,' he heard himself say and listened to his mother's incredulous silence. He used a bit of that silence to form a few more words, to form a few more thoughts, to form a new resolution.

'She's adorable,' he told her. 'Yes, I gave her your ring, and yes, I'd love it if it was on her finger now, but she gave it to Delia because she thinks Delia needs it and wants it more. She's right; Delia should have it. Mom, Holly's adorable. I've never met anyone like her. She's currently wearing a sauce bottle top as a ring as a sort of joke, but come the New Year I want to buy her something permanent. To be honest, I don't know if she'll have me yet but the more I know her the more I know I'll push with everything I can. I would love you to meet her. I'd love it if you could come to Castle Craigie and share my Christmas, meet my Holly and say farewell to this place which treated you so badly but has maybe changed my life for good.'

'You really want me to come?'

'Yes.'

'And you've fallen in love?'

'I think I have.'

'Then don't talk about pushing,' she said, suddenly urgent. 'Don't you dare. She really gave the ring to Delia?'

'She thought it was rightfully hers.'

'It is, too,' his mother said thoughtfully. 'I never thought of it, but...your father really was a frightful man. He had charm by the bucketload but he was emotionally empty.'

'I know that.'

'So this Holly...'

'She's not emotionally empty.'

'And you?' his mother demanded. 'I've often thought...'

'That I'm emotionally empty?' Angus demanded, remembering all those accusations that had hurt so much. But then he thought that maybe he had been. If so, it was from years of practice, though, and years of training. Head, not heart.

But now wasn't the time to recall the past. Now was simply the time for saying it like it was.

'When Holly's around all I seem to feel is emotion,' he said simply. 'Mom, the ring thing…we did it to persuade Delia to let her kids come here for Christmas. Holly's my pretend fiancée, but I'm hoping…well, you know what I'm hoping. Come and meet her and see why.'

'I'm coming,' his mother said. 'I'm on my way!'

CHAPTER TEN

HOLLY AND HER grandmother had planned a Christmas that would live in the memory of those present for ever.

It started at dawn. The great bell attached to the castle chapel pealed all over the valley. The chapel hadn't been used—who knew?—maybe for centuries. Stunned, Angus grabbed a robe and headed out there—and found Holly swinging from a bell rope.

He'd been in this chapel just once on his first tour of inspection. The windows had been boarded up, the place was full of cobwebs and he'd taken one look and backed out.

But now someone had taken the boards from the windows, someone had stripped the cobwebs, someone had dusted and polished.

The tiny chapel was exquisite. The first weak rays of morning sun were shimmering through ancient stained glass. The pews were polished, the flagstones scrubbed and a massive bouquet of wild foliage stood on the altar.

And, above the nave, a girl in crimson pyjamas was pulling the bell rope for all she was worth. It was so high she almost lost her footing as the bell swung to its extremities. She was swinging with it, flushed, beaming—a ridiculous, red-headed urchin with her eyes full of mischief.

'Merry Christmas,' she gasped as she saw him. 'I thought this was the best way to get you up. There's egg nog and pancakes, and porridge for Dougal, and even pavlova because Mary said that's Delia's favourite food and I want her to eat something for breakfast. A week out of hospital and she's still as weak as a kitten. I'm so glad we have two nurses. But Angus, it's going to be a huge day and if I don't get breakfast into you all soon it'll be time for Christmas dinner and think of the waste! So up an' at 'em, Castle Craigie.'

She hauled the rope again and the force of the great brass bell almost lifted her off her feet.

She was irresistible. He wanted to walk forward and take her into his arms. Instead he walked forward, caught the rope and took over the pulling. 'You'll wake the entire valley!' he said but he kept pulling. The great booming chimes were echoing all around them. Christmas, here, now, they said—and something else. The pealing in of a new chapter of his life?

Including Holly?

'Excellent,' she said and plumped down on the nearest pew, giving weight to his new realisation that bell-pulling was harder than it looked. 'Santa believers will be up anyway and if you don't believe in Santa, you should.'

'Why did you clean the chapel?'

'We wanted to. Your mother and I did it yesterday when you took the kids out sledding. She remembered it. She says she used to come here and sit when she was at her loneliest. We snuggled Delia up in cushions and rugs and she supervised.'

'My mother and Delia…'

'Apparently Delia was a scared housemaid when your Mom was here. Now they seem the best of friends. Your Mom even approves of me giving her the ring.'

She did. What was happening here was truly astonishing. Helen had arrived ready to be appalled, but no one could be appalled for long in the Holly-and-Maggie Christmas Castle. They'd transformed it and those who arrived were sucked right in. The Castle was almost full. Dougal was here with his nurses—and with Scruffy-Mac permanently glued to his knee. Delia was here with her astounded mother. The kids and Melly the cat were here, whooping, whooping, whooping, filling the Castle with their life and laughter. Teasing Angus. Being bossed by Holly. Making this place a family home.

As his mother had walked into the Castle, Holly had swooped on her with joy. 'You must be Helen. We are so, so happy that you've decided to come. I need to tell you before you come an inch further in that I've given away your ring, but please don't hate me.'

Any reservations Helen might have held had died right then. She'd been given the old Earl's room but Holly and Maggie had redecorated in a fashion that took her breath away. She'd come down to dinner that night in her customary elegant black but Polly and Mary had looked at her in astonishment.

'Why are you wearing a black dress?' Polly had demanded, ten years old and obviously not one to keep her feelings to herself. 'Everyone's pretty except you. Okay, Maggie wears black but only when she's being boss of the world as Castle Housekeeper. She wears pretty at night.'

Maggie had choked on her champagne and there'd been general laughter. His mother had smiled it off too, but, to Angus's astonishment, she'd made him take her into Edinburgh the next day. She also rejected the twinset and pearl place. She'd come back with colours.

His mother had been wearing colours for six days now, not quite as vibrant as Holly's but almost, and Angus, who couldn't remember his mother wearing colour ever in his life, was astounded every time he looked at her.

It was down to Holly. His miracle-maker.

He tugged the bell while she got her breath back, the great bell rose and fell, rose and fell; he looked down at the girl at his feet…

'I didn't buy you a diamond for Christmas,' he said before he could stop himself, before he could even think that this was hardly the place, hardly the time. 'But I wanted to. I still want to. Holly, I'm laying ghosts all over the place and, employer or not, I can't wait. As soon as the shops open after Christmas, can I take you in and make it official? Holly, I know I hired you as my temporary fiancée, but the position's now been declared permanent.'

She didn't reply. Maybe she couldn't because the

bell was still ringing out and it seemed vitally important that it keep ringing. Maybe he was afraid
that if he stopped there'd be silence, and into that
silence would come refusal.

'You're pretty amazing,' she said at last between
peals and he paused and there was a hiccup in the
ringing but she shook her head. 'No. Not everyone's up yet. Keep pulling.'

'I believe,' he said between pulls, 'that I've just
proposed. I think I need to go down on bended
knee.'

'Don't do that.'

'Holly...'

'Yeah, I know you want to,' she said, almost
thoughtful. 'It's dumb. This feeling between us...
it's like a spell. Neither of us thinks it's sensible...'

'Why isn't it sensible?'

'Well, I'm broken-hearted for one,' she said, and
he had to strain to hear above the peals. 'Practically jilted at the altar and robbed of all my
worldly goods as well as my pride. If I said yes
now it'd be on the rebound.'

'Would it?'

'I think so,' she said cautiously, and it was too
much; he released the bell rope and the great bell
slowly swayed to silence. He sat down on the

pew beside her and she turned to face him. She looked…puzzled. Was puzzled how a woman was supposed to look after a proposal of marriage?

'I'm scared,' she said but she didn't look scared at all.

'Why?'

'Because I don't trust myself? Because this feels like a Cinderella story? Because I've made one ghastly mistake already—and I knew Geoff for years before I agreed to marry him, so how can I fall for you in two weeks? My parents died and I felt…empty. When Geoff left I copped that emptiness all over again and how can I expose myself to that sort of hurt again?'

'I wouldn't…'

'I don't know you wouldn't,' she said inexorably. 'What do I know about you other than you had a fiancée once you hate to talk about and you're scared you might be like your father?'

Those qualms were reasonable. He could answer them—except the last.

The last made him feel ill.

'I was engaged to Louise when I was twenty-one,' he said. 'She was after a rich husband. I was young and dumb. I was humiliated to the core, which is why I don't talk about it, but Holly, a love affair at twenty-one might just possibly be classified as irrelevant now. But for the rest… If you think I might possibly, remotely be like my father then you should run a mile. But it's irrelevant, too. I'm not the Lord of this castle. It's not who I am. I'm selling and running.'

'It's not just the Lord thing.'

'I think it is,' he said roughly. 'Every one of the long line of title-holders has lived in this place and lorded it over their minions. I'm going back to New York, Holly. I'm renouncing the title and all it entails. I'm going back to who I was before my father died, and I want, very, very badly, to take you with me.'

'You can't go back to who you were before your father died,' she said, still looking puzzled. 'You're different. Like me… I'm a whole different woman to the woman Geoff dumped. I doubt myself now.'

'Don't doubt me,' he said, strongly now, taking her hands in his and holding. 'Holly, I don't have doubts. I know it's fast, but you're wonderful. More than wonderful. Marry me and come and live in Manhattan. Bring Maggie if you like. I'll set you up in a restaurant. You'd be amazing— Manhattan would love you.'

'Have you been into my egg nog?' she demanded. 'I know I have. I had to get up and make it so of course I've tried it while I was stuffing the turkey. So now I'm sitting in an ancient chapel in red pyjamas and I've had two lovely swigs of egg nog and you're here making too-much-egg-noggy statements. Angus, this is crazy.'

'This is true.'

'No. It's nuts. And I'm cold,' she said inconsequentially and she shivered to prove it.

He started to haul off his robe but she stood and backed away.

'Cold feet,' she said, but he looked down and saw her gorgeous thick furry boots, courtesy of her finally located luggage.

'Figuratively,' she said. 'Inside, I'm all a wobble.'

'Does that mean you're turning me down?'

'Not...' Still that puzzle remained on her face. 'Not yet. Not today. But I'm not saying yes, either.'

'Holly, I am not my father,' he said steadily. 'I swear. We will leave this castle behind.'

'What your father was about was never about the castle.'

'I think it was. My mother's here making a pretence at keeping cheerful but I see her staring at these walls and I see her shudder. The ghosts here could never let us be happy. Besides,' he said, smiling, 'Manhattan's warmer. Anywhere's warmer than Scotland in winter.'

'So it is, but Scotland in winter's where we are and where you're proposing,' she said. 'And it's where I need to make up my mind. But if I'm not to serve breakfast in red pyjamas then I need to run. You've employed me as a chef as well as a fiancée, Lord Angus, so now I need to put my chef hat on and let Christmas run its course.'

He'd never had such a Christmas. Even the surly Stanley was seen to smile. Holly and Maggie had woven Christmas magic, and if the new owner of the estate turned out to be someone who'd raze the castle and turn it into a golf resort then so be it, the castle was going out in style.

There was so much food—magnificent food. Everyone was groaning by mid-morning but still fronting up for Christmas dinner and then still staggering to the tea table.

Angus felt weird but fantastic, Lord of all he surveyed, head of a sort-of-family that he'd never known existed. At Holly's insistence, he stood at the head of the table feeling almost out of body, carving a turkey that looked as if it had been on steroids. How had Holly managed this? For a start, how had she managed to find such a turkey, because she swore—to the always-enquiring Mary—that it was both free range and organically farmed.

Not that Mary would have suffered if she hadn't been able to eat turkey. The vast table was almost groaning, and Angus looked around at his strange mix of assorted guests and tried to figure how Holly could have them all mixing, laughing and happy.

Because that was what they were, right down to Scruffy-cum-Mac and Melly the cat.

There was Christmas music all around them. Ben was apparently a techno whizz and Holly had put his talents to use, even if as a self-respecting adolescent Ben thought woofers and sub woofers and associated coolness were wasted on *Jingle Bells*. His pay-off was that every fourth song was one of the ones he'd been recording with his mates.

There were games inside and out, and there were gifts for everyone.

Angus hadn't thought of gifts—or he had but Holly had just groaned when he'd mentioned it

on Christmas Eve and chuckled and said, 'Thank
heaven the world doesn't depend on men to keep
it running.' The gifts were small but awesome—
dumb games, movies of old comic-book charac-
ters. And cup cakes, individually designed, each
an exquisite work of art personally designed for
the recipient. Even Stanley got a kick out of his, a
cup cake with a clever construct of Stanley with
his ancient tweed cap and his great hook nose
somehow softened to make him look fun.

Holly…

Holly.

When had he fallen in love with her? he wondered as the day wore on and he watched the life
and laughter surrounding her. When had she bewitched him? For bewitched he was. She might
still have reservations, but he had none. If she'd
accept him, he wanted this woman with him for
the rest of his life.

He thought of his life in Manhattan, as it had
been and as it could be. This joy and laughter for
ever. Was it greedy to want it to start now?

Maybe he shouldn't have asked her this morning. Maybe he'd rushed it.

No matter. He'd just keep asking. She'd lose her
scruples the moment he got her out of this castle,

with all its memories. This place was nothing to do with him. His father's history was nothing to do with him. Without this castle, she could fall in love…

Patience. Time.

'Oi. We're going outside to make snow angels and then we're taking plastic bags up the hill and riding down. You want to come or you want to stand daydreaming into the fire all day?'

It was Holly—of course it was Holly—bundled up like a snow bunny, her cheeks already glowing in anticipation of the cold.

Merry Christmas, Holly, he said silently to himself as he shrugged on his coat and prepared to follow Holly and the whooping kids. 'Every Christmas will be merry now that I've found you.'

Take your time, she told herself. Don't let yourself believe you've fallen in love. He's rushing you. He wants to marry you before he even knows you.

But... There were two Holly voices in this conversation, each as strong as the other. *But he's heart-stoppingly gorgeous. He'd kind, he's gentle, he's rich...*

Since when was rich important?

If all other things are equal, rich is very handy,

thank you very much. It'd be soooo nice to be out of debt.

You'd let him pay your debts?

I might.

That's immoral.

So I have an immoral streak. Get over it.

This internal conversation was doing her head in. She should be concentrating on steering her plastic bag but, try as she might, the plastic bag took her exactly where it wanted. Soft snow was mounded at the bottom of the run; she knew she'd end up buried so she might as well chat as she went.

You've fallen in love; you know you have.

And that's why it's so important to keep your head. Otherwise you'll end up as a kept woman in some Manhattan apartment and you'll be in as big a mess as his mother was.

He says Maggie can come too. That's hardly the action of a man intent on isolating his lover.

Yes, but that's a con. Take Maggie away from her beloved Scotland? He knows she'd never leave.

So what will she do?

What will you do?

Whumff! She hit the snow bank head-on, and in

she went, buried to her ears in soft snow. The kids, who'd learned quickly the skill of hauling back on their bags to avoid the ignominy of burial, hooted with laughter, but a gorgeous man in a kilt strode across, reached out his hands and hauled her out.

She came up too fast. She was too close.

She was breathing far too hard.

'You're a very bad driver, Ms McIntosh,' he told her, smiling down at her with that smile that made her toes curl.

'I'm bad at lots of things,' she managed, now totally breathless.

'You'll fit in fine in Manhattan. Wait and see.'

'No, you wait and see,' she retorted. 'Angus…'

'Yes?'

'Just wait and see. Please.'

She couldn't sleep. It had been the most wonderful Christmas of her life. She'd worked harder than she ever had, she'd played harder, she'd put more thought into gifts, she'd worried more about who was enjoying themselves, she'd set herself a target of sending everyone to bed happy and she thought she'd succeeded. Old Dougal had gripped her hands before his Christmas-sated nurse had helped him to bed and said, 'I don't even mind going back to that place now. I'll remember this forever.'

Forever might not be for very long, she thought, remembering the old man's frail handshake, but right now he was in bed happy, probably asleep, and so should she be. She was happily exhausted. But...

But what?

But nothing. She pushed back her covers and padded across to the long slit window through the two-foot thick stone walls. The moonlight was playing on the snow. In the distance she could see the twinkling lights of the village—did everyone have a Santa Claus on their chimney?

'God's in his heaven, all's right with the world,' she murmured, and it was, but sleep was far away.

She'd loved Angus today. He'd thrown himself into Christmas heart and soul. He'd played dumb games with the kids, he'd seemingly made everyone happy, he was a host whose kindness spread to each and every one of his guests.

Christmas had been wonderful because of Angus.

Angus...

She'd go and check the ovens, she told herself, feeling desperate that sleep wouldn't come and her dreams only had one direction. A Liege Lord in a kilt to die for...

No! Ovens, she told herself fiercely. She'd discovered the huge cleaned-up range was fantastic for bread-making but it needed to be stoked and damped down for the night and she hadn't quite got the hang of it. She could just go see...

She shoved her feet into her furry boots and headed downstairs, pleased to have purpose behind her insomnia—and her errant thoughts. But then...

Angus was in the hall. He had his back to the great hearth, where the yule log smouldered and where lesser logs burned with dancing flames.

He looked up as she came downstairs, but he didn't smile. It was almost as if he was expecting her.

'I'm...I'm going to check the ovens,' she said, struggling to make her voice work.

'Maggie and I already checked them. Maggie says they'll be perfect for your bread.'

'I...thank you. I'll go back to bed, then.'

'Holly...' And all of a sudden he was right there, right at the foot of the stairs and a girl should turn and run but there was no way in the world this girl was turning and running. Not now. Not on this magic night. Not when this man was standing before her, looking like…

Like he loved her?

Every sense was screaming be sensible at her, but there was something below, something so deep, so primeval that sense didn't stand a chance. Angus was right here, right now, and yes, a sensible woman should back away because she'd made a lot of very sensible resolutions and so had he, but suddenly there didn't seem to be an ounce of sensible left in either of them.

'Angus,' she said stupidly and he smiled and took her hands and drew her to him.

'Holly,' he said and it was as if wedding vows were spoken with that word. Love, honour, commitment—somehow she heard them all. Maybe it was wishful thinking, maybe it was pure fancy, but her head was no longer responding to instructions. This was pure heart. This was pure, instinctive need.

For this was her man and he was holding her, needing her and she wanted him as she'd wanted nothing else in her life.

'Come to my bed,' he said as he kissed her hair and drew her closer, closer and her body melted, just like that. She had nothing left to fight with and who wanted to fight anyway? This was her lord, her love, her gorgeous, gorgeous Angus, and he wanted her and she ached for him and nothing else mattered.

'You're already wearing my ring,' he told her. 'I love that you're wearing it, but it involves a promise. You're not my paid fiancée, Holly McIntosh, you're the woman I want more than anything else in the world. I'd give you my castle, my kingdom, my heart. I do give them to you. Holly, I love you and I want you in my bed. I want you for the rest of my life. I'll take a no if I must but if you could possibly see that scrap around your finger for the gold it should be...'

'I think I do,' she managed, somehow getting her voice to work. 'I'm sure I do.' And she wound her hands around his body, tilting her face to meet his, feeling his arms enfold her, lift her and finally carry her in triumph up the sweeping staircase to the vast lordly bedroom beyond.

'I do,' she whispered as he pushed the door open with his foot, as he carried her across the bedroom, as he laid her with all reverence on the huge four-poster bed and then sank down beside her to gather her in to him. 'Oh, Angus, I do, I do, I do.'

CHAPTER ELEVEN

THE TIME BETWEEN Christmas and Hogmanay was magic. Time out of this world. A fairy tale. For those within the castle walls, the rest of the world might not have existed.

And the way Holly looked at Angus, the way Angus looked at Holly, was just perfect.

'They're such a wonderful couple,' Delia said, over and over again to anyone who'd listen. 'I never thought I'd see a Lord of Castle Craigie who knew what it was to love.'

'He's my son,' Helen said fondly, seemingly finally reassured. 'He's nothing like his father.'

But, strangely, Maggie wasn't so certain. She watched her granddaughter with eyes that held reservations, but by the end of the week even she was being drawn into the fairy tale. Or Angus and Holly were trying to draw her in.

'You'll come to Manhattan with us,' Holly said and she'd managed to laugh.

'I won't, but we'll worry about that in the New

Year. This is like the Cinderella story, with mid-night being the day after Hogmanay. For now, let's soak up the ball.'

'It won't end,' Holly said stoutly. 'Gran, he's wonderful. He's not the least like his father. You must be able to see it.'

But, *I don't see him giving much,* Maggie thought. *Yes, he's being generous but Helen says he can afford to be. In the end he's talking about taking my girl back to his castle, to his Manhattan. You show me a Lord that gives and I might believe it.*

She didn't say it, though. Holly was in a bubble of love and laughter, and for this time, for this magic season, she wouldn't burst that bubble. She could only hope that the bubble was an old woman's worried fancy, and Holly's happy ever after was solid, loving fact.

'Angus is so much fun,' ten-year-old Polly exclaimed as she swooped past, freshly baked muffin in her hand, on her way from one Very Exciting Adventure to another. Angus had organised ice skates and they were off to try their skills on the shallow pond behind the chapel. 'But Holly's awesome, too, and Angus has wrapped Mum up in blankets and she's there waiting to watch me skate. This place is like magic. Even Mum says it's magic.'

And she was gone, enthralled with her fairy tale, leaving Maggie with her faint doubts and her desperate hope that she was wrong.

'I hope it's me being paranoid,' she muttered, but then she knew…what Holly didn't know. She hadn't explained it to her before the job came up, and afterwards… Would Holly have taken the job if she'd known? Probably not.

'But it shouldn't make a difference,' she told herself. 'He has every right to do what he's doing.'

But maybe it did make a difference. The more she saw of Angus's wealth, the more she thought it.

When she'd pushed Holly to go to London with him she hadn't thought through the ramifications. Almost as soon as they'd left, those worries had surfaced and they were on the surface still.

So tell Holly?

She'd figure it out. In time.

Would she mind?

Oh, Holly… Maggie thought, deciding that Holly might mind very much.

'I'll tell her after Hogmanay,' she told herself. 'After her Cinderella midnight.'

* * *

Hogmanay. Holly and Maggie had put more effort into this than they had Christmas, and they had the entire Castle population behind them. Even the children had worked. This was the party to end parties, the farewell of the Castle to the village. Everyone was seeing it as the landmark it was.

'It's the end of a long line of appalling landowners,' Angus said in grim satisfaction. 'I've had an offer from an Arabian oil tycoon. I'm heading to Glasgow on Wednesday to sign. He'll turn the place into a magnificent hunting and golf resort and the old Lords of Castle Craigie will be nothing but a dim memory.'

On the surface it seemed perfect.

But…

Maggie watched the preparations and knew she wasn't the only one feeling desolate, but it wasn't her way to show self-pity, not on such a day. They had the old place gleaming. They'd been cooking for days. The kids had built a bonfire to end all bonfires. They'd organised games for all ages. Holly had even attempted to make enough haggis to feed all.

Maggie watched the villagers come, she watched

their awe at the transformation, and she thought: what if…? What if…?

What if nothing. Angus was selling and moving on, as was his right. He'd take Holly with him as was his wish.

The Lord of Castle Craigie had the last word.

It wasn't until the bonfire was lit, until the first leaping flames had died down a little and Holly stood among a group of weary, food-and-fun sated villagers that she realised there was sadness.

She'd been watching the flames. She turned and the two women closest to her were hugging each other, and one was weeping.

Who knew why? Maggie knew these people but she didn't. It wasn't her business to enquire.

But she'd spent the past couple of weeks making people happy. These tears seemed wrong.

'Can I help?' she enquired gently of the two women. 'Would you like me to take you into the Castle, show you to somewhere private?'

'I…no, thanks, miss.' The dry-eyed one was suddenly moist as well. 'It's just…it's going to be so hard. We got the final notices yesterday.'

'Notices?'

'Vacating requirements,' the woman said. 'Two

months. Mr Stanley says that's more than generous but it's still heart-breaking. We've been here all our lives. It's fine for them who can afford to buy, but so few of us can. With the latest financial crisis, even those of us with good paying jobs can't get credit to buy. Craigenstone's finished. Your Gran... Us... This day marks the end. It's the first time in living memory the Lord has celebrated Hogmanay, that he's acted like a Laird instead of a Lord, but isn't it fitting that he's celebrating being shot of the lot of us?'

And Holly's mind turned to stone, just like that.

The sale of the Castle. *Craigenstone's finished.*

Oh, my...

Her head was whirling, trying to grasp facts, and the facts she saw looming up out of the abyss were appalling. And it was as if the abyss had been there all along, but she hadn't looked. She hadn't seen it. She hadn't even glimpsed it.

How could she have been so blind?

Gran hadn't told her.

But she had. Her head was sending her back three weeks ago, to the day she'd arrived.

'The landlord's selling after all these years. I should have saved, but Holly, somehow I never dreamed... What a stupid old woman.'

She'd heard Maggie say it and she'd felt ill, but she'd imagined one landlord, one cottage. Not an entire village.

'What...what do you mean, acting like a Laird and not a Lord?' she managed and one of the women gave a short, humourless laugh.

'A Laird is Himself,' she said. 'He's the keeper of the estate, the one who cares. We've never had one here and now we never will. We've always had a Lord, but what good is that to us? Nothing at all, and now less than ever.'

They turned away, distressed, and Holly was left on her own. She found her feet wandering aimlessly to the back of the bonfire, away from the crowds. She needed space.

She needed sense.

She was Australian. She hadn't seen the picture, but now...she'd read enough historical novels to get what was happening.

The estate wasn't just the castle; it was the whole of Craigenstone, and an oil tycoon buying an estate to form a hunting/golf resort would want as many of the picturesque stone cottages as he could get. It sounded as if Angus had offered to let the villagers buy theirs if they wanted—if they could afford it—but the remainder would go in the sale.

She saw Stanley standing a little apart, with the same grim stance as he'd always had. She didn't like the man. She knew Angus was only putting up with him because there was no one else who knew the place, but still, he gave her the creeps.

Now she forced herself to go forward and talk to him.

'How many cottages are being sold to their tenants?' she asked him directly and he didn't even bother turning towards her to answer.

'Ten.'

'Out of?'

'Sixty. The buyer would have taken them as a job lot but His Lordship insisted tenants be given the option.'

'Nice of him,' she snapped and something inside her snapped too.

When she thought of what this Christmas had cost there hadn't been a quibble. She'd looked Angus up on the Internet; he'd even shown her. He was part-owner of one of the biggest financial institutions in the world.

Christmas here would be a drop in the ocean of his wealth. What he'd get for this village would be nothing in his vast financial ocean.

But he wanted to be shot of it. While he owned

the Castle he was compared to his father; he was Lord of Castle Craigie and he didn't like it.

So why not sell it?

He was selfish, just like Geoff, she thought, feeling sick to the heart. How could she have been so blind *twice*?

Her feet were still acting of their own accord, finding their way seemingly all on their own to the back of the crowd, where he stood, a tall, solitary lord surveying the scene he'd created.

She'd thought she loved this man. She'd given him her body. And her heart?

No! Head, not heart. Had she learned nothing?

'Angus...'

He turned and saw her and he knew at once that something was wrong. His brows snapped down in a frown. 'Love?'

'I'm not,' she said carefully, 'your love.'

'That's not what you said this morning.'

'This morning,' she said carefully, 'I didn't know you were evicting an entire village.'

'I'm not,' he said, startled.

'You're selling the estate. The entire district of Craigenstone.'

'I am, but...'

'But what?'

'But it's time it stopped being feudal,' he said gently. 'This Hogmanay might well be in keeping with centuries of tradition, but a Lord has no place in these people's lives. You know that. All I'm doing is moving into the twenty-first century.'

'All you're doing is going home to Manhattan.'

'That's unfair.' His dark brows had snapped down. 'Holly, these people don't want me. They didn't want my father or my grandfather before him.'

'Maybe they did, but they didn't get them.'

'I don't know what you mean.'

'I mean this village is gorgeous,' Holly said. 'It's ringed by mountains, it's freezing in winter, it's probably invaded by midges in summer, yes there are downsides, but even I can see that this is a community, not a collection of individual cottages. And a community needs a leader. Yet you're going to make a fortune and walk away, leaving these people with what? Golf?'

'With their own homes.'

'Not with their own homes. Ten out of sixty are buying. The rest are leaving.'

'That's their choice.'

'How can it be their choice? How dare you say that?' She was practically yelling. 'With the global financial crisis in full swing, how do you expect someone like Gran to get a loan? Her parents, her parents' parents and parents' parents' parents lived in this village, right next door to the cottage she lives in now, and as a bride she moved next door, to where her husband's people had done the same. They've never been offered the choice to buy, so they've never thought of it. And now, pow, eviction, and off they'll go to some welfare housing in the city. If they're lucky.'

'Would you keep your voice down?' he said and, to her fury, he sounded amused. The bonfire was still crackling. The bagpipes, which someone had been playing in the background, had died while everyone watched the flames so Holly's fury could be heard. 'Holly, it's not that bad. If anyone really wants to stay, they can.'

'How?'

'I've organised finance. I have it available. If your Gran or anyone like her wishes to stay in their cottage then they can. The rent they're paying now will cover the interest. It's an interest-only loan, not repayable until they move out, or in the case of direct descendants, until the next generation moves out. Then the cottage will be sold and the loan called in at point of sale. Villagers can elect to sell any time they want—no pressure.'

'That's not what Gran told me.'

'It's what I'm telling you.'

'Even if it's true, it's still splitting the village; you're still killing a community.'

'That's nothing to do with me,' he said, but as she looked at him she saw a faint trace of unease. This night—or, more, this gathering in the Castle over Christmas—must surely have shown him how important community could be. 'Holly, the feudal system is dead. I can't be expected to stay here as Liege Lord, the same as my father.'

'So you're acting as ruthlessly as your father would have: abandoning them, heading off to Manhattan to make more money...'

'That's not fair.'

'Why does Gran have to sell her house?'

'She doesn't.'

'She does. She doesn't have a choice. And why is Edna Black crying? Why is Essie McLeod sobbing along with her? Why is this whole community disintegrating while you make money?'

'Holly...'

'Head, not heart,' she said, and the anger had suddenly gone. 'The acorn never falls far from the tree. Dumb Holly, that's me. And blind. Geoff robbed just me but you're robbing a whole community. I can't believe I've been so stupid. You are like your father.'

'How can you say that?'

'So why are you going back to Manhattan? Your father would have done exactly what suited him. Isn't that what you're doing? I don't know the ins and outs of finance, but I know Gran is destitute—that's why I was forced to work for you. Right. I've worked for you. I've been your chef and your fiancée for Christmas and beyond, but Hogmanay is now over. My official contract finishes tomorrow, just as soon as I've done the washing-up, stripped the beds and put back the dust covers.'

She wrenched—with some difficulty—the crazy metal ring from her engagement finger and handed it back. He took it without a word.

'Sense prevails,' she said dully, stepping back. 'I've made one stupid, stupid mistake, I walked straight into another and I'm done.'

'Holly, I love you.'

'Well, I don't love you,' she said and gave the lie to her words with a sob. 'I can't. Angus, I want heart and that's all I want. I know this is dumb, but somehow I want the whole fairy tale. I want a man who truly knows how to be a Lord. A Laird even.'

Holly disappeared—to the kitchen? To start the washing-up? To cry her heart out? He desperately wanted to follow, but first he had to get some facts.

Half an hour talking to villagers gave him an outline. Yes, he should have talked individually to his tenants before, but he'd been here such a short time, enough to see his father's neglect, the contempt in which his father was held. He'd thought he'd pack up and leave as soon as he could. Only Ben's phone call—and then Holly bursting onto the scene like a Christmas angel—had interfered with his plans.

So as far as the sale went, he'd left the communication with the villagers to Stanley. Stanley was in charge of the rent roll. He knew each of the villagers individually, so Angus had worked out his terms and left it to Stanley to talk to them.

But now it seemed Stanley hadn't talked to them—he'd written. One of the villagers who lived closest heard Angus's tight-lipped questions and nipped home fast. He came back with two letters.

Angus read, and a cold fury started burning deep within. Was that an oxymoron? Cold and burning? But that was what this felt like. He felt ill.

Holly's accusations were just.

He'd left this to Stanley. He knew Stanley was guilty of petty dishonesty, he didn't like the man, but it had been so much easier to leave it with him.

Why had he done what he'd done? He paced, and paced some more, and then he made a couple of calls. To the agent in London who specialised in large estates, who'd been handling this sale, who was earning so much from it that he didn't mind taking a call at this hour. And then to the Middle East, to the accountant of an oil tycoon.

Then he went and found Dougal. The old man was still awake. He'd been out in his wheelchair, watching the bonfire. Now he and his little dog were propped up in bed watching the dying embers through the window, watching the villagers drift home, watching the end of the estate.

He was astonished to receive his late night visitor, but in half an hour Angus realised the man's mind was still razor-sharp and coldly vindictive.

Towards Stanley and towards Angus's father, who'd employed him.

'He told me Mac'd been given a home by Rob at the pub,' he said as a parting shot. 'Lying hound. He just booted Mac out. I don't know how he's survived. As far as Stanley was concerned, we were both better off dead.'

It was a fitting epitaph to the accusations whirling in his head. His father. Stanley. Himself. Some of those accusations were aimed squarely at him.

Then he sat down in silence in the Castle library and stared bleakly into the night.

You're killing a community.

It was a cold thought and it was absolutely true.

What to do? How to repair such damage?

Not sell? The contract wasn't irreversible. But if he didn't sell… He'd seen the cottages, the roads, the infrastructure. He'd seen the grinding poverty. The place needed a massive injection of… something.

Love?

Holly?

That was crazy thinking. He had to think like a financier here. A financier was what he was.

He was also Lord of Castle Craigie. It was a role

he didn't want, he'd never wanted, but that was what he was.

A Laird as well as a Lord? Somewhere, in the night's conversations, that distinction had been made crystal-clear.

Finally at dawn he rose and walked to the gilt mirror over the fireplace. A bleak figure looked back at him, unshaven, tired, grim. He was still wearing the kilt of his forebears. He was dressed in the Highland battledress of ages.

So… He was the Lord of Castle Craigie ready to face barbarians from without, but it seemed the barbarians were within. This battle was nothing to do with the oil tycoon who'd offered to buy this place. It was a little to do with Stanley. Soon, when he had his facts fully together, he'd go and face the man.

But it had everything to do with himself.

He wasn't like his father.

He wasn't, he thought grimly, and he knew, he just knew, that given this current set of facts the old man would have walked away without a backward glance. What the oil tycoon was offering was truly staggering.

But Holly would expect…

Holly did expect, and so did he. He cast one last

look at the letters, at the figures, and something within him settled into a rock-hard resolve.

He needed to talk to Stanley, he thought. Now.

And then he needed to talk to Holly. If she'd listen.

CHAPTER TWELVE

HOLLY HAD CRIED herself to sleep. This was dumb. It was the behaviour of an angsty, lovesick teen-ager. Even when Geoff had done his worst she'd felt anger and disgust and distress but she'd never sobbed into her pillow over him. Over humiliation, yes, and over desperation at her financial position, but never over Geoff the man.

But last night—or in the wee hours when she'd finally cleaned up the kitchen—she'd crept up-stairs and hauled her blankets over her head and given way to despair—a despair only matched by the loss of her parents. Her grief seemed to go that deep. Bone-deep.

She'd been so tired and so distressed she hadn't so much as combed her hair. She knew she had ash on her face, she knew her eyes were swollen from crying, she knew she was a sodden mess and when the knock came at the door she dived under the covers and yelled, 'Go away.'

Then she peered out from under the covers again and checked her bedside clock. Seven. She'd crawled into bed at four. Three hours' sleep.

But her contract said she still had to work today—her last day. Did the hordes want a cooked breakfast?

She would do this, she thought determinedly. She would fulfil her contract and take the money promised her. Then at least Maggie would have enough for a rental bond.

Something good had to come from this mess.

'Breakfast in half an hour,' she yelled to the knocker. 'Go away.'

Instead the handle turned and the door opened inward.

Angus.

She should have locked the door.

The door didn't have a lock.

She should have wedged the chair against it. She did not want this man in her room.

Angus.

He hadn't slept. She could see that at a glance. He was exactly as he'd been last night, in full Highland regalia, smoke-stained, five o'clock shadow and then some, tired, strained, grim as death.

'We need to talk,' he said, but she shook

her head and sat up, hauling her bedclothes to her neck.

'There's no need. What's done's done. I'm finishing up at lunch time. Everyone's leaving. You and Stanley can do your worst.'

'You think I'm an ogre, don't you.'

She took a deep breath, trying to see sense, trying for a bit of justice here. This man hadn't asked to inherit. He didn't want this place. He'd come, he'd sold, and he was moving on.

Oh, but the pain he was causing...

'Stanley's been taking a cut,' he said, slicing across her thoughts. Jumping right in where her thoughts were centred. He hadn't come into the room—he was standing at the door as if he had no right to come further.

'Stanley,' she said cautiously, trying to fight back judgement for a moment. Let the accused speak...

'I can't lay it all on Stanley.' His words were as bleak and hard as his face. He stood against the door-jamb as if he were in the dock admitting murder. 'But it is my fault. Back in Manhattan I'd never have let an unknown employee have such responsibility, especially one I already suspected of dishonesty, but here it seemed I had no choice. I came over to settle the estate, sell it and get back to Manhattan. Stanley was the only retainer left who knew the place. I gave instructions but they weren't followed. That's up to me. I suspected the man was dishonest; I just hadn't dreamed how much.'

'What's…so what's he done?' She could barely get her voice to work. She wasn't inviting him in. She wasn't lowering her bedclothes from around her neck. Bedclothes and distance were fragile armour but they were all she had.

'He took a kick-back from the buyer's financial men,' he said. 'He gets ten per cent of the value of any cottage included in the purchase. Stanley knew he had to communicate my offer to let each cottager buy, but he failed to mention the financial help I'd organised. So therefore every cottager was faced with a two-month eviction notice unless they could find finance on commercial terms. In this climate…'

'Financial help? You were offering…what?'

He told her. He stood and watched as she listened. He watched as he saw her thinking of the offer, how much it would have meant to Maggie, how much it would have meant to every cottager struggling to come to terms with leaving.

But she still didn't lower her bedclothes.

'It's better,' she said at last. 'I mean, it's good. So, now you know, you'll fix it?'

'I'll fix it. Stanley's sacked and already gone. I hope to never see the man again, but my lawyers will be following him. No contract's set in stone yet. Every cottager who wants to stay will be able to.'

'Great,' she said. 'That's that then.'

'Yes.'

Fantastic, she thought. Justice had been served. Maggie could stay. The village of Craigenstone would go on being Craigenstone. She should be whooping.

She wasn't.

'So you'll reorganise the cottage sales and go back to Manhattan?' she asked dully.

'See, there's the thing,' he said, gently now, as if he'd only just figured it out for himself but was afraid to say it aloud. Afraid to make it real. 'I don't think I can.'

'Leave?'

'No.'

'Wh…why not?'

'Because this estate needs a Laird.' And then he smiled, a tired, rueful smile, and he glanced down at his smoke-stained kilt, his sporran, all the trappings of his title. 'Maybe it needs a man the villagers can refer to as Himself. Someone who cares. This estate's been run down for generations. I spent a lot of last night talking to McAllister. It's amazing how awake he can be when his passion's firing and, at the first talk of estate restoration, fire it did. His body's failing but his mind is razor-sharp. One hint from me and orders came thick and fast.'

'Orders?' Her bedclothes had slipped now, just a little, not so much as you'd notice, and she wasn't noticing. She was too busy listening.

'This valley has no industry at all. There was a woollen mill on the estate until thirty years ago, but it fell into disrepair during my father's time. It needed massive upkeep but my father closed it rather than spending money, and its loss caused untold poverty for the crofters. Apparently our sheep produce the finest fleeces in all of Scotland. The reputation for our product remains to this day, but the land's been let go to ruin, the crofters forced off the land by poverty, the market ignored. If I was to put in some decent infrastructure…restore the crofts…build more cottages rather than sell…put money back into restoring our flocks for fine wool…McAllister says there's enough of our sheep left to pull the flocks back together. He also says there's enough of the skills remaining in the old folk to get the mill restarted. Craigenstone Woollens. We might just make it work.'

'But Angus, you're talking years,' she said, trying to get her head around what he was saying. 'You're talking…passion.'

'Yes. And I'm talking staying here,' he said. 'I'm talking about not being like my forebears. I'm talking about bringing this valley back to life.' And then he paused. 'I'm talking life, my Holly. Here. With you. With the kids if they want to stay, and it seems right that they do. With McAllister behind me for as long as he's able. I'm talking about forever.'

'You've decided this in one night?' She was so breathless she could scarcely get her words out. 'How can you have decided so fast?'

Still he didn't come near. Maybe he didn't think he had the right. Maybe he thought she'd scream the roof down. 'Because it's been a long night? No,' he corrected himself. 'It's been a long three weeks. Three weeks to change a life?'

'I don't know what you mean.'

'Can I come in?'

'Yes, if you don't touch me,' she managed.

'Are you scared of pillaging?' He threw her a weary smile, and that smile…it made her world turn inside out.

'Angus, I'm scared of me, not you,' she admitted. 'Up until yesterday, my hormones were going nuts for you and yes, they still are, and you're still wearing that kilt and your legs are doing my head in, but I made my decision last night and I'll stick to it.'

'Even if my parameters have changed? Even if your accusation that I'm just like my father shoved something home that should have been shoved home years ago, and has been the catalyst for massive change. Holly, your accusations are just. Maybe my mother's fears have been just. I live for myself—I always have. I don't try to do harm. I put my head down and work and I make a lot of money, but I've never thought of the bigger picture. Or maybe I should make that the smaller picture. The financial corporation I run gives a lot to charity. I give when I'm asked, but I don't give because I see need. That's obviously because I don't look.'

'But you did look when Ben asked to come

here,' she admitted. 'You did ask Dougal to come. You've filled the Castle.'

'Yes, but that was because you were here,' he said bluntly. 'When I advertised for you I didn't even want you. If I hadn't found you I would have had an excuse not to have the kids here. I didn't give myself.'

'So...so now what?' she managed, and finally he walked forward, he moved to her bedside but he didn't touch her. He was still keeping his distance. Employer speaking to employee who'd thrown accusations at him and quit.

'I've fallen in love with you, Holly McIntosh,' he said softly into the stillness of the morning. 'More. I've fallen in love with what you are, and it's what I want to be. I want to be able to give like you do. I want to be able to live like you.'

'What, fall in love with rubbish men?' she demanded, and he smiled.

'You've fallen in love with one and a half rubbish men. The final half has redeemed himself. Or intends to redeem himself. Holly, think about what we could do with this Castle. Think! We could turn this place around. Craigenstone would come to life again. I have the capital to inject. I'd love to do it; I will do it. Holly, if I need to, I'll do it alone, but I don't want that. I've fallen in love with my wonderful Christmas gift, my Holly, my girl who's turned my life around.'

'You…you don't want to go back to Manhattan?'

'I'll need to go back and forth from time to time,' he conceded. 'The company's running smoothly but I'll still need to maintain my interest to fund what we need to do here. But…you've never been to Manhattan.'

'No.'

'Would you like to go?' And then, before she could speak, he put his hand up. 'Don't answer. Not yet. I'm not asking for a Manhattan bride. I'm asking for a bride for Castle Craigie. I'm asking for a Lady for a Lord, a Herself to match Himself, a woman who'll help make this Castle, this whole estate, truly grand. And who'll occasionally accompany her husband on his business travels—when he really needs to be away and when he can't bear to be parted from her.'

'Angus…'

'Because I can't bear to be parted from you, Holly,' he said softly, putting his fingers on her lips, and then he stooped and took her hands gently into his. 'I love you, Holly McIntosh and I'll do whatever it takes to make you love me. If that means every time I go to Manhattan I need to take along three kids, their mum, your gran, a dog, a cat, Dougal, his nurse, this whole amazing entourage, then so be it, but my days of being a loner are over. I don't want to be Lord of Castle Craigie alone, my love. It's quite a title and it needs to fit us all. I think Lord should be another word for family. Lord of Castle Craigie. Us.'

And then, as she failed to speak—for how could she speak when her eyes were wet with tears?—he tugged her forward and she felt the last of her armour slip away. He tugged her into his arms and he held her, as if she were the most precious thing in the world, and Holly McIntosh's world changed right there, right then.

Her Lord had found his Lady. Cinderella had found her prince.

Holly had found her Angus.

'Will you marry me?' he said, the words muffled in her hair and somehow she managed to nod. It was a pretty weird nod, though, when she was so close, so close…

'Yes,' she managed.

'And will you love me?'

'Of course I'll love you,' she said through tears. 'I love you forever, forever and forever. I wanted to. I thought I did the first time I saw you, especially in that kilt, but Angus, I didn't trust...'

'You had reason not to trust. But can you now?'

'Maybe,' she said between kisses. 'Maybe, my love, as long as you keep wearing that kilt, maybe I know I can.'

It was a great day in the history of the tiny village of Craigenstone when Lord Angus McTavish Stuart took one Holly Margaret McIntosh to be his bride.

They were married in the chapel of Castle Craigie—of course they were—but the chapel was tiny and there wasn't a soul in the district who didn't want to be part of this joyous day. Marquees had been set up with sound and vision so this wedding could be shared by all.

'She's our girl,' the villagers declared, conveniently forgetting Holly's father had gone to Australia and married an Australian and Holly spoke with a broad Aussie twang. For this day she was Our Maggie's granddaughter, a local, their girl taming the Lord of Castle Craigie.

For Angus was still the Earl of Craigenstone. No one wanted him to renounce the title. The villagers saw Angus taking on the title as a beginning of a new and bright future, not a continuance of the same.

He was moving mountains, this new Lord of theirs. Their Laird. Already an army of workers was repairing roads, restoring long neglected cottages, preparing crofts for the sheep that Angus planned would return to bring prosperity back to the valley. The old ways had been superseded by the new but there were many who craved quality and craftsmanship, and Angus's business acumen saw a niche that wasn't small.

The mill was being rebuilt. The old folk of the village were being turned to for advice, for teaching. The village hummed and there was already talk of young ones, drifted away for generations, returning to take part in this new resurgence.

And it all hung on this couple, this darkly handsome Lord, who looked just like his father but who wasn't the least like him, and his astonishing half Scottish, half Antipodean bride.

And now the day had come. Angus stood before the altar in his wedding finery—the Stuart tartan, the dress sword, tassels, sporran, every piece of Scottish gorgeousness Holly could convince him to wear. Dougal was in his wheelchair by his side, looking almost as fine, waiting with his Lord for the woman who'd made this happen.

Holly.

And here she was, rounding the great Castle walls in a dray. Maggie was by her side, dressed to the nines as well—someone had to use that Very Expensive Dress Shop in Edinburgh—and she was giving the bride away, for there was no way in the world she was letting another do it.

The dray came to a halt. Holly jumped down almost before it stopped, not waiting for the dozen men who'd surged forward to help. Mary and Polly collected her train—vintage lace because this was Maggie's gown recycled, but there was nothing recycled about this bride.

She looked exquisite, She was exquisite. Angus thought, as he watched his bride make her way towards him. The deep cream gown fitted her to perfection and her copper curls glowed and glinted in the afternoon light.

She'd always glow, he thought, and somewhere in his heart he felt room to be sorry for the unknown Geoff, who'd treated her so badly and in doing so had given Angus, given this valley, these people, so much.

'I've got your ring safe,' Ben whispered as Holly

grew nearer but Angus didn't hear. He had eyes only for his bride.

From this day forth…

They'd fill the Castle, he thought, with their family, their friends, their animals. They'd make this place a home as it truly should be a home. It might be a great grey fortress on the outside but on the inside… Holly had brought her heart to this Castle and it was transformed.

More, she'd brought her heart to his, and that was transformed as well.

'My love,' he said softly as she reached him and he took her hand and drew her to stand by his side. 'You look beautiful.'

'You don't scrub up too badly yourself,' she said and grinned and he chuckled, a lovely deep chuckle that had every lady in the congregation sighing and knowing exactly why it was that Holly was marrying this man.

But Holly knew more. She wasn't marrying him for his smile or his laugh. Nor for his Castle, his title or his money.

She was marrying him because he was her Angus; it was as simple as that.

She smiled up at her husband-to-be, a lovely

heart-warming smile that was as much of a match for his chuckle as it was possible to make.

'No laughing. This is serious,' she said softly. 'You've promised me a gold ring and that's what I'm here for.'

'You won't give this one away?' he asked and her smile died.

'I won't,' she said, and her eyes met his and he knew what she spoke now was absolute truth. 'This one's for ever.'

* * * * *

Mills & Boon® Large Print
April 2014

0314 Rom LP

Mills & Boon® Large Print

May 2014

THE DIMITRAKOS PROPOSITION
Lynne Graham

HIS TEMPORARY MISTRESS
Cathy Williams

A MAN WITHOUT MERCY
Miranda Lee

THE FLAW IN HIS DIAMOND
Susan Stephens

FORGED IN THE DESERT HEAT
Maisey Yates

THE TYCOON'S DELICIOUS DISTRACTION
Maggie Cox

A DEAL WITH BENEFITS
Susanna Carr

MR (NOT QUITE) PERFECT
Jessica Hart

ENGLISH GIRL IN NEW YORK
Scarlet Wilson

THE GREEK'S TINY MIRACLE
Rebecca Winters

THE FINAL FALCON SAYS I DO
Lucy Gordon

Discover more romance at

www.millsandboon.co.uk

❤ WIN great prizes in our exclusive competitions

❤ BUY new titles before they hit the shops

❤ BROWSE new books and REVIEW your favourites

❤ SAVE on new books with the Mills & Boon® Bookclub™

❤ DISCOVER new authors

PLUS, to chat about your favourite reads, get the latest news and find special offers:

🅕 Find us on facebook.com/millsandboon

🐦 Follow us on twitter.com/millsandboonuk

❤ Sign up to our newsletter at millsandboon.co.uk